# THE DARKNESS WITHIN

# THE DARKNESS WITHIN

THE MIRRORED CROWN: BOOK 3

JESSICA R. LEMORE

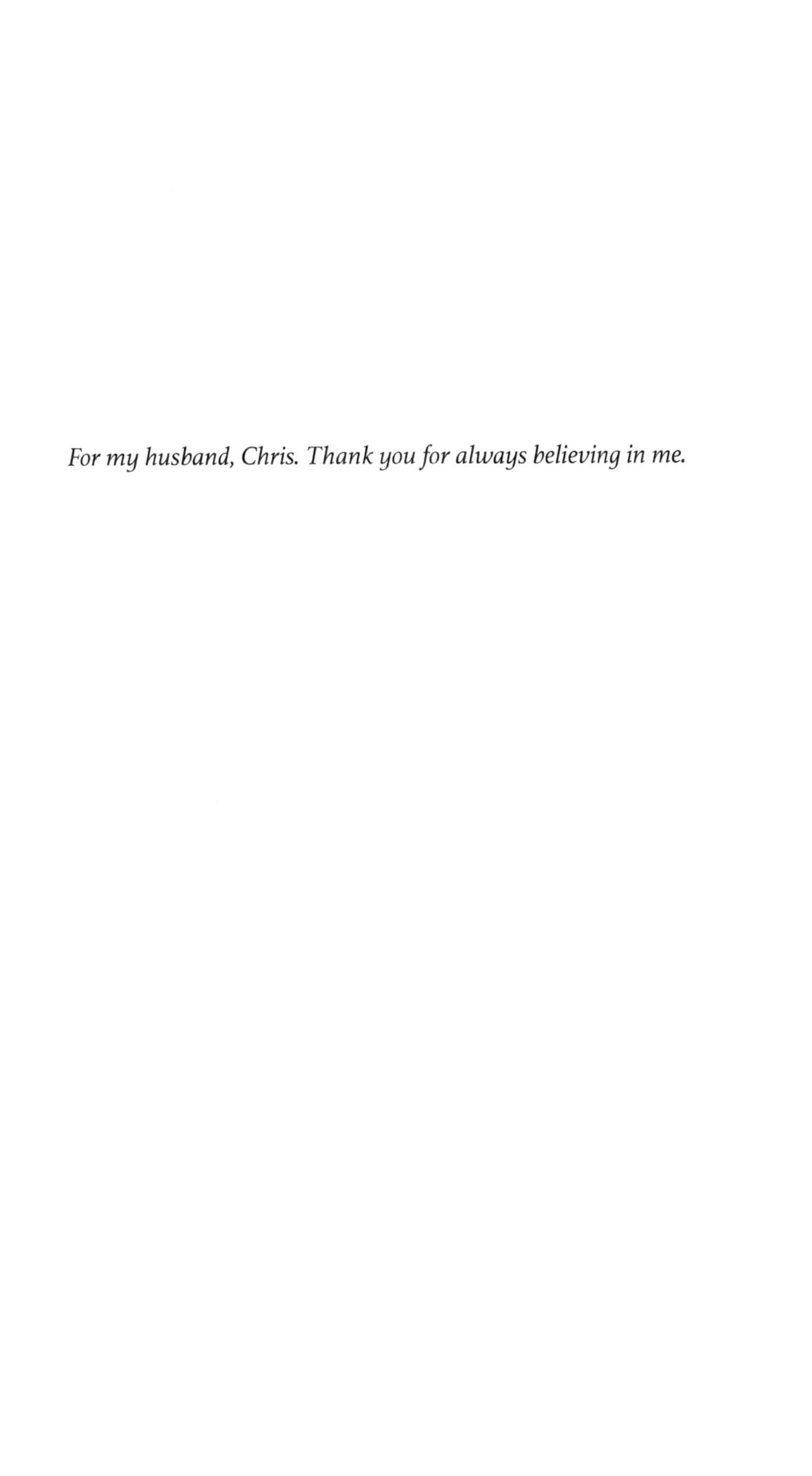

*For my husband, Chris. Thank you for always believing in me.*

# CONTENTS

# PROLOGUE

King Mathias leaned back, resting his head on the plush throne. The sharp sting of exhaustion overtook him, and his eyelids involuntarily flickered, the exertion to keep them open finally overtaking him. They had only been shut for a moment, but it was enough to see a woman kneeling on the ground, her hands clasped before her and her eyes wide. A moment later, a dark shadow fell over her. The woman collapsed, a deep guttural scream overtaking the silence.

When he opened his eyes, a long sigh escaped his cracked lips. His hand flew to his forehead as he rubbed the vision out of his mind. With each passing second his eyelids grew heavier, as if protesting the lack of sleep.

The visions hadn't become any easier. It had been eight months since they began. Eight months since *they* had been called into his world. Eight months of famine, pain, and destruction. As soon as they were released, he knew he had made a mistake. He had been foolish, arrogant even. A pit formed deep in his belly. All he had wanted was to see his son again. Drunden's death may as well have been his own. Everything good in the world had vanished. He should have listened to the Revatto's warnings.

He closed his eyes again, and a memory sprang forward. As the last drop of blood slid across the smooth surface of the dagger, the portal opened. Where he had been expecting to see his son, a dark void appeared. The shapeless figure stepped into the light. Three more followed in quick succession. Before he could move, more figures followed, too many for him to count.

The sound of heavy footsteps in the hall broke him from his memory. A shiver passed through him as the hair on his arms prickled. He listened to the footfalls, counting them. When they ceased, his mouth ran dry as the door slowly creaked open, revealing a large shadow. A line of pure white frost crept across the room, devouring everything it touched. The air instantly chilled as the shadow spread.

Adrenaline shot through him, and he sat up, elongating his spine. As the frost slowly made its way to the foot of the throne, he lifted his head high, meeting the hard gaze of his guest. A tall man stepped out from the shadow, his face pale, and his jaw hard. His dark, empty eyes swept across the room.

King Mathias held his guest's gaze. His nostrils flared at the man's silence, a spark of anger igniting.

"What more do you want? What more can you take from me?"

His visitor stepped forward. When he was before the king, he spread his arms wide, inhaling deeply.

"You called me here," he said, his voice deep. "How can you be angry when you invited us in?"

King Mathias gripped the throne tightly, trying to remain calm. The demon fed off of fear. He didn't want to make them stronger. It was his fault his land was suffering. His fault his people were suffering. If something didn't change, if they weren't stopped, nothing would be left.

"What do you want?" King Mathias remained calm. "Are you finally here to kill me?"

"Why would I kill my gracious host?" The demon took another step closer, the frost pooling at his feet.

King Mathias threw himself onto his knees, the pain radiating up his calves. He clasped his hands before him. "Leave Medora. Go back to your home, your world. Leave what's left of my people alone."

The demon smiled, his lips curling upward, revealing sharp white teeth. "That's why I'm here. If you want to save your remaining subjects, bring us more."

King Mathias shook his head slowly. "No. This has to stop."

The demon turned, following the line of frost into the hallway. "The decision is yours."

King Mathias let out a deep breath. The line of frost faded, melting into the floor. He used the silence to think of a plan, something to send them back to their world, their dimension. Killing them wasn't an option. He had tried multiple times. No dagger or poison worked on them. They were invincible...but he wasn't.

King Mathias stood. He wrung his hands, trying to clear his head. He had called the beasts into his land. He had opened the door, invited them in. They thanked him by killing everyone around him, his subjects. He saw their last moments, the visions haunted him day and night. He was connected to them. There was a reason they hadn't killed him.

It was in that moment he knew what he had to do. He reached into his cloak and withdrew a large silver dagger. The same dagger that had been used in the sacrifice eight months prior. He wasn't sure his plan would work but it no longer mattered. He couldn't bear to see his city fall.

He closed his eyes and pictured Drunden. His heart swelled as the memories beckoned him. When the sharp blade pierced his skin, he fell to the ground, his right arm pinned underneath his body. Bright red blood pooled around him. His last thoughts centered around the monsters he had so carelessly let into his world. He only hoped his plan would work and they would be sent back to their land, their home, and that no one would ever be so foolish to call on them again.

**1**

---

## THE DEMONS

The darkness within Lana was spreading, rooting itself to her. Ever since she had returned to Bridian, after destroying the Crystal, her life had changed. A line had been crossed. One that she could never come back from.

A splash of water drew her attention, and she lifted her head from her bent knees just in time to watch a monogrose jump into the air, snapping its sharp teeth. She had been sitting near the large floor-to-ceiling window for hours, calling them. As it fell back into the water, she smiled, amused with her newfound ability.

She had discovered the talent by accident. When the voices became too much, when their cries couldn't be silenced, she went to the one place she knew she would be left alone. The small room had a view of the stables, and was nestled in the back of the castle, in an area no one ventured. It had been her sanctuary. The large window overlooking the moat became her amusement as she watched the beasts in the water. The first few times she had called a monogrose was easy to pass off as coincidence. By the fifth, she knew it was her—the demons.

Lana leaned against the wall and closed her eyes, but too many images haunted her thoughts to keep them shut for long. She wished she could fall asleep, even if for only a few minutes, but couldn't bear to relive the memories. Every time she shut her eyes, she relived the night she found the Crystal. She remembered Terris's mother, pinned against the wall by a file cabinet. She blamed herself for Shandra's death. Terris repeatedly told her it was for the best, that Shandra would have killed them if Lana hadn't stopped her, but the way he looked at her had changed. He no longer sought her company.

Lana longed for the normalcy of her life in Mt. Sinclair. She missed the anonymity of being a normal teenager. Her life veered off course when she learned her parents weren't her parents. She was really a princess, and future queen of Bridian. She had been in hiding for fifteen years from her father, Alderic, and his rebels. Her grandfather had imprinted the location of his son's weapon into her mind before his death, and Alderic wanted it back.

As she thought of the Crystal of Medora, she realized how foolish she had been. The demons had been imprisoned within it during a ceremony to release them into the world. She thought she would have been strong enough to destroy it and send them back to where they came from. Too late, she realized how wrong she had been.

While she had been able to destroy the Crystal, the demons that had been imprisoned inside were another story. Even now she felt sick to her stomach as she thought about them. She wished, more than anything, that they would leave her. At this point, she didn't even care where they went.

"Are you going to dinner?"

Grant stepped into the room and crossed his arms over his chest. He watched her, waiting for her answer. She was glad that he was still assigned to guard her; although she knew that even he wouldn't be able to protect her from herself when the demons finally overpowered her.

"No. I'm not hungry."

He frowned. He watched her for a moment, almost as if he wanted to say something, but thought better of it. She smiled when he turned around and stepped back into the hall, glad that she was alone again.

Lana twirled her ring around her finger. It had been Kalinia's before her death. Tiny, delicate leaves wound their way around the band. Her mother loved leaves and would spend hours looking at them. Although Alderic's initials were also engraved on the inside of the band, she still cherished it.

The sound of horses beckoned her to look out the window again. A carriage pulled away from the castle. Had Ramos received an answer from the Council? He had petitioned the Council of Elders to question Amos, Terris's father. Before he had been imprisoned in Bonawickham Yards, Amos believed there was a way to transfer the black magic out of Lana and into himself. She hoped there was a way to not only transfer it, but the demons as well. The problem was, the Yards is highly restricted. The Council doesn't allow any visitors. Ramos was hoping that their unique circumstances would work in their favor and the Council would grant their request, but she was tired of waiting.

Lana shivered as darkness clouded her vision. The demons were restless. When her vision returned, she blinked, letting her eyes adjust to the sudden light. She still wasn't used to the darkness that overtook her and didn't think she ever would be.

When she heard the screech of a monogrose she knew it was time to leave. They were fighting with each other. She stood, brushing the dirt off her cloak. She liked it when they fought and wanted to stay and watch, but knew it was only the demons inside her that liked the conflict. She turned her back to the window and took a deep breath to steady herself before walking into the hall.

Grant jumped up from his chair, surprised to see her. He had to be bored since she began spending all her time alone. Without looking at him she made her way to the stairs.

"Did you decide you're hungry after all?" he asked hopefully.

"No, I'm just going to my room."

He sighed but didn't say anything else. She was careful to avoid the dining hall. She didn't want to see her parents, Ramos, or her cousins. She didn't want to feel pressured to eat with them. She didn't want to be around everyone in the crowded dining hall, so she stopped going, preferring her meals to be brought to her room. After a few days of this, her parents began forcing her to join them for every meal. She only lasted two days before breaking down during lunch. She had spent the entire hour crying about everything from the demons to the cold chicken on her plate. After that, she had been given a reprieve but knew it wouldn't last long.

When she stepped into her bedroom, she closed the door behind her. She took another deep, calming breath and leaned against the wall. She wished she had somewhere else to go, somewhere no one knew her. Maybe she would be able to start fresh somewhere else? As soon as the thought came, she dismissed it. Would anyplace be safe from the demons?

Lana made her way to her bed and fell into the soft mattress. She looked at the delicate lace hanging from the ceiling and imagined how different her life would have been if Nick Jacobs hadn't tricked her into walking home from school. If she hadn't been attacked, she would probably still be living in Mt. Sinclair, completely oblivious to Alderic and his Rebellion.

A low thumping began in her ears, slowly spreading to her forehead. She curled her fingers into the blankets as her body trembled. When the demons settled, she let go of her blue daisy quilt and stood. The lights flickered as she made her way to the mirror above her dresser. Pitch black eyes stared back at her.

When they settled, she took a deep breath, trying to steady her nerves. They were getting stronger. How long would it be before they finally overpowered her?

**2**

———

# THE COUNCIL'S DECISION

Lana dreamed of the Mt. Sinclair Welcome Center. Bright red blood poured out of her eyes as the Crystal shattered all around her. It slid down her face, falling to the floor, and pooling at her feet.

Her hands flew to her cheeks when she awoke. Relief washed over her when she didn't find blood. She ran her fingers through her hair as she steadied her frantic breathing. Would the nightmares ever end?

The early morning light crept in through the window. Outside, birds were chirping, and soldiers ran their drills. A yawn escaped her lips. She didn't want to fall asleep again. She couldn't handle another nightmare.

She walked to her dresser, finding a pair of dark blue jeans and a purple sweater, the sleeves outlined in a thin black lace. She had a few clothes from Mt. Sinclair and still wore them, not wanting to give up every aspect of her old life. She laced her sneakers and threw her curly hair into a messy ponytail.

Lana wished she could reverse time. If only she could have gone back to Mt. Sinclair before she found the Crystal. She should have known she wouldn't have been strong enough to send the demons away. Her stomach twisted at the thought that she had not only let her family down, but the citizens of Bridian as well. She knew she had to get past the disappointment and deal with the consequences rationally, but she felt helpless and didn't know where to start.

Suddenly, she had an idea. She had wanted to go back to the abandoned hall, but Ramos had the mirror leading there sealed. But it didn't matter now that she could teleport. She closed her eyes and imagined the room, hoping she remembered enough detail to take her there.

When she felt the swish of air around her, she opened her eyes and smiled. She didn't think she would ever really get used to the fact that she could just think of a place and be there instantly, and then remembered the downside. There was a chance that someone powerful enough could pull her to them. Memories of Medora flooded her, sending chills down her spine.

The room looked exactly as it had the last time she had been there. Everything was covered in dust and the drapes were ripped. She ran her hand along the wooden throne before her. When she sat down, she imagined what it had looked like fifteen years ago.

Before she knew the truth, that she was a princess of Bridian, she had been plagued by the same dream. She later learned that the dream had actually been memories given to her by her grandfather before his murder in this very room. She remembered how beautiful the room was, and for a moment pictured it as it had been.

The jeweled map hung above the door, the rubies, emeralds, and sapphires surrounded by gold. The thrones were polished, and the large windows sparkled, the red velvet drapes pristine. When the vision faded, she stood and walked to the enormous fireplace. When she was standing before it, she reached out and touched the cold stone, tracing the outline of the dragon. Her fingers stopped at the indentation of the dragon's eye, where the pearl that Terris used to wear around his neck should have been. He had been given the dragon's eye as a clue to the Crystal's hiding place by her grandfather and Lana wished that she had not solved the mystery so soon. If she hadn't recognized the pearl around her friend's neck as belonging to the dragon on the fireplace, perhaps the Crystal would still be safely hidden.

She crawled through the grating of the fireplace. When she was in the tiny room she sat down on the cold floor and pushed her knees to her chest, wishing she could stay hidden forever. It had been unfair that she had so much responsibility thrust on her. She didn't want to be Queen of Bridian. She didn't even want to be a princess.

She made her way out of the fireplace when her stomach started to rumble. She looked around the room one last time, memorizing every detail. When she was ready, she closed her eyes and imagined her bedroom. Tendrils of hair fluttered around her face. A moment later, she was standing next to her bed. She nervously twisted her ring around her finger and opened the door, her lips curving into a fake smile when she saw Grant.

"Good morning," he said happily. "Did you sleep well?"

She nodded, closing the door behind her. She prepared herself for the crowd in the dining hall. She really didn't want to eat with everyone but needed to see her uncle. The curiosity was eating away at her. Had it been a Council carriage she had seen yesterday? If it hadn't, perhaps she could persuade him to ask again. She was tired of waiting. If she had to join everyone in the dining hall for an answer, she was willing to try.

"It's nice to see you going to breakfast," Grant added.

Lana stopped walking. Was she really ready for this? Was she ready to try again? Maybe if everyone gave her space it would be easier. She turned to look at him.

"Do you think you can keep everyone away from me?"

He chuckled. "I have a feeling the prince and princess would have me banished if I tried to keep them from you."

Lana sighed. She hoped she could handle the attention. It would be worth it if her uncle had good news from the Council. Before she knew it, she was standing before the dining hall doors. She took a deep breath when she heard laughter. The sound was jarring. It frayed at her already fragile nerves. Grant stepped next to her and pushed the door open before she changed her mind.

The room fell silent. It looked as if every seat was taken. All eyes turned to her and even though she had been expecting it, it still felt uncomfortable.

"I'm so glad you're joining us," Ramos said, standing from his chair at the head of the table.

Lana smiled weakly before making her way to her usual seat between her parents. As she traversed the room, the whispers began.

"Is it safe for her to be here?" someone asked, their voice low.

"Of course, it is," another voice carried. "That's our princess."

When she sat, Jacqueline leaned close. "I'm so proud of you. I know this isn't easy."

Lana sank into her chair, hoping everyone would go back to their meal. She didn't want to be the center of attention. She didn't want to be talked about. Most of all, she didn't want everyone's pity. The lights flickered and she inhaled deeply. Jacqueline took her hand and squeezed it. Deliah waved at her before turning back to her food.

A plate was set before Lana, filled with ham, eggs, and a slice of warm buttered toast. She reached for her cup and took a sip of the Choclochino, trying to blend in.

"Deliah, move your chair," Dominic said, his eyes narrowed at his sister. "You're too close to me."

Deliah shrugged. "This is where I always sit."

Lana scanned the room, looking for Terris and Trevor and saw them sitting near each other, next to Nick Jacobs and his family. When Trevor sensed her gaze, he whispered to Terris. *What were they talking about?*

She watched Mr. and Mrs. Jacobs for a moment, wondering if Mr. Jacobs was happy to be back in Bridian. To her surprise, Kiernan was conversing with Mrs. Jacobs. He usually sat with his father, but a quick scan of the room revealed that Langdon wasn't there. Kiernan turned to the person sitting to his right.

*Marnie*, she thought bitterly.

Lana knew she had no right to be upset. She hardly talked to Kiernan anymore. She went out of her way to ignore him, partly because she didn't want to hurt him. But the biggest reason she had been avoiding him was the awkwardness of their last conversation.

Marnie leaned close to him, and Lana pushed her plate away. She had to leave. The energy in the room was too much. Between Kiernan, and everyone watching her, she felt sick. Even though she recognized her emotions were all over the place, that this wasn't her, she couldn't stay. She would talk to her uncle another time. This had been a mistake. She stood, but before she could leave, a hand reached out to stop her.

"Are you all right?" Jacqueline asked.

Lana nodded. "I'm fine. It's hard to be around everyone."

Jacqueline's eyes searched hers, making her uncomfortable. It always felt as if she could read her mind.

"We'll get you in a bit," she said a moment later. "Grayson and I want to take you somewhere."

Grayson's seat was empty. He was talking to Grant. She was sure he was prying for information, learning everything he could about what she had been doing since he had seen her last. She could only imagine how riveting that conversation was.

"Where are we going?" Lana asked.

"Not far," Jacqueline answered. "To the Square."

Lana's thoughts turned back to Grant. What was he being punished for? Guarding her had to be punishment for something big. She only received a guard after she snuck out of the castle to go to Poklin's. Since it had been a punishment for her, it only made sense he was making up for his own transgressions. Did he resent her?

She felt a sharp tap on her shoulder and turned around again, expecting her uncle. Instead, Kiernan stood smiling at her. For a moment, her breath caught in her throat. Then she remembered her time at Willow Manor. She crossed her arms over her chest, rebuilding her wall.

"What?"

He looked taken aback and she almost had a change of heart. She wanted to apologize for shutting him out of her life, but it was easier this way. She couldn't open up again. It was too painful.

"I just wanted to say that it's nice to see you," he said, shifting on his feet. "It's been a while."

His smile fell. Before she had a chance to say anything Marnie joined them.

"Hi, Lana." She giggled, making Lana's insides churn. "I wondered where you ran off to," she added, looking at Kiernan.

Lana pushed her chair back. "I have to go."

Before either Kiernan or Marnie could say anything, Lana slipped out of the dining hall. Her eyes stung with fresh tears, and she wiped them away before anyone could see. When Grant joined her, she made her way to her bedroom, grateful her cousins hadn't followed.

Grant put his hand on the door, preventing her from closing it. "Next time will be easier."

"I doubt it," she said.

Grant stepped back. She ran her hands through her hair. When she turned from the door, her crown caught her eye. She hadn't worn it since she had returned from Mt. Sinclair and hoped she would never have to again. It had been carefully placed on her dresser, mocking her. The light from the window reflected off the diamonds, casting multi-colored rainbows throughout the room.

Her gaze shifted to the mirror, and she studied her reflection carefully, looking for any changes, anything to alert her the demons were winning. She let out a sigh of relief when she saw that her eyes were still brown, not black. The freckle above her left eyebrow was still there and her curly brown hair looked the same.

A moment later, a knock on the door interrupted her thoughts. Jacqueline looked into the room.

"King Ramos would like to see you."

Lana's eyebrows raised. Was this what she had been waiting for? Could he have heard from the Council?

"Has he heard anything?"

She shrugged. "I don't know."

Lana looked at her reflection one last time before stepping into the hall. She followed Jacqueline to the first floor. Grayson was waiting for them. He led them to her uncle's throne room. Two guards opened the double doors, admitting them.

Ramos was sitting on the throne, his head in his hands. A younger man was standing in front of him, holding a scroll. When Ramos heard the doors open, he sat upright. His eyes were red, and Lana immediately knew something was wrong.

"I was hoping I would have better news to deliver, but I'm afraid I don't."

"They've reached their decision?" Grayson asked hopefully.

"You've heard from the Council?" Lana said at the same time. "What did they say? When can we see Amos?"

The young man standing near Ramos cleared his throat. When Lana looked at him, he held the scroll, offering it to her.

"Lana, this is Johan," he said, gesturing to the man. "He's the Council's messenger. You can read it."

Lana took the scroll. When she had it in her hands, she was surprised how heavy it was. She unrolled the parchment and read the tall script.

*King Ramos, Bridian*

*After much deliberation, we, the High Council of Elders, deny your request to visit prisoner 41985, Amos VanDriesen.*

*Respectfully,*

*Lorelle H. Elingston, Gideon D. Astley, Ambelle R. Davenport, Elora L. Haskell, Vernon G. Tilman, Winston Gale, Philomena I. Roset, Genevieve M. Marston, Dalton N. Morley, Franklin O. Perli, Judah M. Livingston, Cecil G. Prescott, Elex Dorsey*

After rereading the letter twice, Lana sighed. She couldn't understand why they were being denied the chance to talk to Amos. Why hadn't they listed a reason for their denial?

"They denied our request," she muttered. "I don't understand, how could they deny it? Why didn't they even give us a reason?"

"They don't need to give us a reason," Ramos answered. "They're the Council."

Lana ran her fingers around the scroll, as if it would give her another answer. "Well, let's ask them to reconsider. Maybe if we appealed, they would grant us permission. We only want to talk to him, it's not like we want to break him out."

"Once the Council makes their decision, it's final," Ramos said. "There is no appeal process."

Her stomach fell. "What are we going to do?"

Her pulse quickened and her head throbbed. Suddenly, the darkness overtook her. The lights surged and she slid to the floor. The demons winning. As she fought to regain control, strong arms wrapped around her, trying to help her stand.

"Lana, you have to fight them," Grayson said. "Come back to us."

The pain in her temple intensified. She tried to suppress the demons, to regain control of her body. When she was about to give up, to give in to them, they retreated, and she broke free.

"What's wrong with her?" Jacqueline cried. "Do something!"

"She'll be all right," Grayson said. "She's coming around now."

When the pounding in her head stopped, Lana opened her eyes. She was lying on her side, facing away from everyone. Beads of sweat dripped off her face. She slowly sat up. When she was sitting, she inhaled deeply, the warm air scratching her throat.

"I thought that was it," she mumbled. "I thought they had me."

"You have to control your emotions," Ramos said. "You almost handed yourself over to them. You can't let them win."

Before she had a chance to say anything, Jacqueline hugged her. Tears streamed down her face as she ran her hands through Lana's hair, as if making sure that she was really there.

"I'm so glad you're all right. Don't do that to us again."

"It's not like I meant to do it," Lana snapped, trying to push herself out of her protective grip.

Jacqueline's lips parted, as if she was going to say something but Grayson beat her to it.

"King Ramos is right." He sighed. "You let your emotions get the better of you and they fed off it."

"So, you're telling me I can't allow myself to feel anything ever again?" she asked, her voice rising. "We need to talk to Amos. We need to find out what he knows. If there's a way to get them out, I need to know."

"Give me time," Ramos said. "Please don't do anything foolish. I need time to think."

"There must be a good reason the Council denied your request," Grayson added. "We have to trust that they know what they're doing."

Lana's jaw dropped. Why was he siding with them? It didn't make sense. She looked around the room, searching for Johan. She had to tell him that she needed to speak with the Council. If she could just talk to them, she knew they would reverse their decision.

"Where is he? Their messenger?"

"I sent him out when you went under," Ramos answered. "I just hope he didn't understand what was going on."

"What do you mean? Why do you care if he knows?"

"I'm sure he'll report back to the Council," he answered, sitting in his throne.

"Maybe that's a good thing," Lana said, hope springing inside of her. "When the Council hears how serious this is, maybe they'll change their mind."

Ramos shook his head sadly. "That's what I'm afraid of. When they hear how serious it is, they may decide you're not safe to be around others."

Lana wondered what that meant. It seemed as if that would be a good thing. She had to show the Council what she was fighting, what she was dealing with. Maybe then they would understand why she was asking to see Amos. When Jacqueline took her hand, the truth hit her.

"Do you mean they'll send me to the Yards?"

When Ramos didn't answer she knew how serious the situation was. She had only been concerned about the demons overpowering her. She hadn't thought that the Council might see her as a threat now, before the demons even had a chance to take over. She shuddered at the thought of being a prisoner.

"What are we going to do?" she asked.

"Give me time to think," Ramos said. "We need to stay positive, and you need to control your emotions."

"Will they be able to take me?" she asked. "The Council?"

"No," Ramos answered. "They need proof. Just make sure you don't give them anything to be concerned about."

A low cry escaped Jacqueline's lips. The room spun, making Lana dizzy. She wasn't sure she had the energy to stand. What would she do if the Council sent her to the Yards? She didn't want to be imprisoned but realized if the demons overtook her, it would be for the best. She didn't want to hurt anyone.

"Everything will be all right," Grayson reassured her. "Don't worry."

Lana wasn't sure how he could tell her not to worry when it felt like her life was falling apart all around her. In that moment, she knew what she had to do. Lana was going to talk to Amos, with or without the Council's permission.

**3**

---

# THROUGH THE ORB

When Lana walked into the hall, a slight tremor passed through her, snaking its way down to her feet. Why did the demons overpower her when Johan had been watching? Why had the Council denied their request? How had her life spiraled so out of control? Her life was crumbling around her, one layer at a time. She felt a hand on her shoulder. She looked up and saw Jacqueline.

"Be strong, Lana. Everything will be okay."

Her parents didn't understand. How could they? Their lives weren't planned out for them—predetermined with no way out. They didn't have the demons inside them. Bridian was, and always had been their home.

"It's okay," Grayson added. "You'll get through this. The important thing is you're here. You're with us. The demons haven't won."

"I can't live like this," Lana said, her hands falling limp to her sides. "This isn't fair. None of this is fair."

Jacqueline reached out, swiping a stray curl off her face. "I know this isn't what you want to hear. Life isn't fair. Everything will be okay though. We're together. We'll get past this, as a family."

"There's a light at the end of the tunnel," Grayson added. "One day you'll see. Each day is a gift. Focus on the good."

Lana sighed. How could she call this a gift? If it was, where could she return it?

"In the meantime," Grayson added, "Let's go to Calyndra's. I think a little fresh air will be good."

Lana narrowed her eyes. Had she heard right? Gareth had opened the shop a week ago. It was all Deliah and Dominic talked about. They both went to the grand opening. Lana had been invited but hadn't wanted to go. The thought of the crowd, the shop crammed to capacity, hadn't appealed to her. She was surprised they wanted to go anywhere in light of the current situation.

"It'll be good for you," Grant spoke up. "You spend all your free time alone."

She quickly turned at his voice. He was standing behind her, his arms crossed over his chest. Ramos was next to him, quietly watching. An uncomfortable silence fell upon them.

"You just want to leave the castle," Lana said, trying to break the tension.

Grant uncrossed his arms. "That would be nice."

Lana pinched the bridge of her nose. Maybe leaving the castle would be good for her? Maybe taking her mind off of her problems, if even for a moment, would help?

"Fine." Her voice cracked.

Jacqueline smiled; her eyes alight. Ramos retreated to his office. Grayson led them down the hall, to the main entrance. Grant made his way to a few soldiers near the door. Her stomach sank, remembering Ander. He died protecting Jacqueline during the attack in Port Morgan...Bridian's youngest soldier.

Lana stopped walking. "Maybe this isn't a good idea. I

should go back to my room. We don't know when the demons are going to try again. We don't know what the rebels have planned. What if they're out there, waiting for the right moment?"

"There are extra patrols in the Square," Grayson said. "It's just as safe as inside. You won't have to worry about that."

Jacqueline turned to Lana. "The more you try to fight it, the more time you spend isolated, the easier it will be for them."

"You need to stay grounded," Grayson added. "The more people you interact with, the easier it will be."

"But we won't force you," Jacqueline said. "If you don't think it's safe, we won't go."

Lana looked at her feet. She didn't think it would be that easy. She didn't think that being around people was the answer. Grant joined them, three soldiers flanking him.

Her parents were waiting for her to decide, to tell them what she wanted to do. She turned the options in her head. Going to the Square may be a nice break, a distraction from her troubles but was it worth the risk? Maybe she needed to leave, stay far away from everyone. A lump formed in her throat, and she swallowed, ready to tell them that she was going to her room when Jacqueline's expression stopped her. Her eyes were trained on her, her brow furrowed.

"Sure," Lana said. "We can try."

Jacqueline's face softened and she took Grayson's hand in hers. "You can buy whatever you want."

Jacqueline's grin lit up the room and Lana knew she had made the right decision. She made her way to the front door. She hadn't really wanted to buy anything. It was the last thing on her mind. She only wanted to make her parents feel better, make it seem like she was back to her former self. The girl whose biggest worry was hoping her crush would notice her. Judging by Jacqueline's reaction, it worked.

When Lana walked over the drawbridge, the monogrose

below followed. She heard movement in the water and resisted the urge to look. She didn't want to draw the others out. She didn't want them to fight. Instead, she kept her gaze in front of her.

The air was warm. The large, bright sun was high above them, reminding her that it was almost summer vacation in Mt. Sinclair. She should have been relaxing, sleeping in, spending her days with her friends. Not fighting the demons inside of her.

Lana looked up at her parents. "Has Trevor's mom been found?"

Her parents were quiet. She knew the answer was no. Trevor wouldn't still be in Bridian, living at the castle if she had been found. She wasn't even sure why she had asked.

"No," Jacqueline finally said. "We're still looking for Heidi."

A million thoughts raced in Lana's already preoccupied head. Where was his mom? Was she still in Mt. Sinclair? Had she willingly left? Did someone do something to her? Her disappearance was very uncharacteristic.

"His dad?" she asked, her voice low. "I know he left them a few years ago, but has anyone tried to find him?"

Grayson sighed. "We found him."

Lana stopped walking. One of the soldiers behind her had been following so close he nearly ran into her. Her parents turned around.

"What are you not telling me?" she asked, her eyes narrowed.

"Nothing," Jacqueline said quickly. "Why would you ask that?"

Lana put her hands on his hips. "If you found Trevor's father, why is he still here? Where is his mom? You know more than you're letting on."

"Let's sit down for a moment," Jacqueline said, gesturing to a small garden partially hidden behind the row of shops. "We can talk in private."

Lana relaxed when she looked toward the Square. Every few yards a soldier was stationed, ready to protect the castle. She followed her parents to the garden. A small fence surrounded the vegetables. Rows of crops lined the rich soil. She recognized pumpkins, lettuce, and squash. A few other vegetables dotted the dirt, but she was too anxious to look at them.

"What's going on?" she asked.

"The Bureau found him." Grayson sat on the bench. "He's in Pennsylvania."

Lana let out a gasp. "That's good news."

"Ken is remarried," her mother said, shielding her blue eyes from the sun. "They have a newborn. He wants us to wait for Heidi. He gave us permission to keep Trevor. In a few days, if she isn't back, he'll take him."

"He knows about Bridian?"

Jacqueline quickly shook her head. "No, he thinks we're still in Mt. Sinclair. If we can't find Heidi, we'll meet him in Pennsylvania."

"The Bureau is looking for her," Grayson added. "It won't come to that. Trevor will be reunited with his mom before you know it."

Lana wasn't so sure it would be that simple. Heidi had already been gone so long. Her disappearance didn't make sense.

"Does Trevor know? About his dad?"

Grayson nodded. Lana's head pounded, the circulation echoing in her ears. Her friends needed her. She had been so consumed in her own problems; she had neglected her friendships. She had to change that, she needed to change.

"Let's go." Jacqueline stood. "The shop's not far."

As they neared the Square, she heard the fountain. Even

though she couldn't see it, she knew it was right behind the building and shuddered. The memory of time freezing, the fear and the confusion it caused, haunted her. Her knees grew weak, but she pushed forward, following Jacqueline.

A light breeze blew past them, making the shop sign rattle. The old Poklin's sign had been replaced. A wooden sign swung in the wind. *Calyndra's Candy* was written in a large, thin font. Lana climbed the stairs.

When Grayson opened the door, they were greeted by the sound of laughter. The shop was full of people, excitedly browsing. Those near the door stopped what they were doing to bow when they saw her.

Lana followed Grayson deeper into the shop, wishing she could blend in. Even without the crown, she was easy to spot, mainly because of the soldiers guarding her. She inhaled deeply, letting the air fill her lungs in an attempt to steady her nerves.

Matte black signs, with silver and gold lettering, were hung on the crisp white walls. Crescent moons, silver roses, and stars decorated the shop. An assortment of silver vases lined the shelves, each filled with a different candy. Playing cards, stationary, and miscellaneous items like pens and pencils were nestled between the sweet treats. A large shelf was to their right, decorated with various crystals of all shapes and sizes. A small peach-colored stone caught her eye and she walked to the shelf, admiring it, the light reflecting off the many facets. The crystals were beautiful, so different from the demon-possessed stone that haunted her nightmares.

"How nice to see you, Princess Lana," a voice called, rising above the laughter.

Gareth stepped out of his office. He smiled before bowing.

"We missed you at the opening."

Lana nodded, her eyes darting around the shop. "It looks so different."

He chuckled. "Yes. Won't you sit?"

Gareth led them deeper into the shop, toward the long bar. Bright sunshine poured in from the window overlooking the Square. Outside, the fountain sat. When she turned from the window, she made her way to the bar. Jacqueline and Grayson joined her, while Grant and the other three soldiers stood behind her, blocking her from others in the shop. The bar was polished with a thick, clear varnish.

"What would you like?" a young man asked.

"On the house," Gareth said.

Lana searched for a menu, a sign, anything that would give her the options to choose from, but there was nothing to be seen. "Any tea is fine."

The man nodded.

"I'll have the same," Jacqueline said.

Lana placed her hands in front of her. A large sign on the wall caught her attention. *The point is happiness* was written in silver metallic ink. Underneath the words was an arrow, pointing to the right, drawn with the same silver ink.

"My mother's mantra," Gareth said when he noticed her looking at the sign.

"What does it mean? I don't get it."

Gareth's eyes focused on the sign, as if lost in thought. "She always said that happiness is the point of life. Our job is to seek it out, to create it, even in the most trying of times."

The man behind the bar set a large teacup in front of Lana. Steam curled out of the glass, swirling into the air. Small silver roses decorated the cup.

"That's her handwriting," Gareth added. "She passed on five years ago. The shop is named after her."

Lana brought the cup closer, her hands flinching from the heat. "The roses? Do they mean something to you?"

Jacqueline's tea was placed in front of her. Grayson leaned over the bar to speak to the server over the noise of the patrons.

"They were her favorite flower," Gareth answered. "I'm from Arleyth. The silver roses are native to my home."

"They're beautiful," she said.

Jacqueline turned in her seat. "What brought you to Bridian? Arleyth isn't close," she added, looking at Lana. "It's far, across the ocean."

"I came here as a young boy," he answered. "With my father on vacation. I fell in love with Bridian. It was magical. The land is gorgeous. The grass is greener. Arleyth is desert—hot and dry."

Lana turned to her parents. "Roses can grow in those conditions?"

Jacqueline leaned back in her seat. "These are a different line of roses than what you're used to in Mt. Sinclair."

"Arleyth's roses thrive in those conditions," Grayson added. "They don't need much water, hardly any."

Lana brought the tea to her lips, flinching from the heat of the cup again. She determined it was still too hot to drink yet and placed it on the bar. While she waited for it to cool, she drummed her fingers on the table. When Grayson cleared his throat, she turned to look at him.

"While we're here," he began, looking at Gareth. "I just want to finalize a few things. Can I have a word in your office?"

Gareth's eyes went straight to Lana. His forehead furrowed slightly before turning away. He swept his right arm out, gesturing Grayson ahead of him. Lana stood and reached for her tea.

"We'll wait here," Jacqueline said, placing her hand on Lana's. "King Ramos asked us to check in with Gareth about an upcoming event. There's no need for all of us to go. Enjoy your tea."

"I'll be right back," Grayson added.

Lana narrowed her eyes. Even though the exchange seemed odd, she didn't really want to be involved. She sat down and continued drumming her hands on the counter when the voices began. They were calling her name. She closed her eyes tight, her eyelid muscles throbbing from the pressure.

"Lana." Jacqueline leaned close. "Are you okay?"

Lana nodded, hoping that no one else had noticed her change. She opened her eyes, desperately trying to ignore the voices. The lights flickered.

Jacqueline placed her hand on her arm. "Trevor seems to be adjusting well. Did you get a chance to visit him today?"

At the mention of her friend, the voices stopped. Lana relaxed, the tension in her forehead fading.

"Drink your tea," Jacqueline added. "It's delicious."

Lana couldn't think clearly. Maybe the tea would help. Maybe the distraction would clear her head. As she reached for the cup, another thought took root. How was she ever going to live a normal life again? Why did she think it was safe to leave her seclusion?

Her hands shook as they reached for the cup. A slight tingle radiated through them, shooting through her palms, and extending to her fingertips. She watched as a thin line of frost made its way across the bar top to her cup, climbing up the side.

Lana's mouth opened, her lower lip trembling as the thin crystalline frost made its way over her cup and down the other side. She brought her hands to her face, looking for any indication that the frost had come from her.

"Let's go," Jacqueline said, placing her napkin on top of the frost, covering what she could. "Grayson will meet us outside."

Lana stood. It felt as if she was in a daze, or a dream. Had the frost come from her? It had originated from her side of the bar. Where else would it have come from? Deep down she already knew the answer, but it still didn't seem possible.

Jacqueline turned to the man behind the bar, talking softly. Grant escorted Lana out the front door. She carefully made her way down the steep steps into the Square, her mind racing. What other abilities were going to manifest? Would she ever be able to control them? As the strange occurrence replayed in her head, the confusion dissipated, pushed to the side by excitement. A smile graced her lips as she wiggled her fingers. She had done that. She had made the frost. What else could she do?

"Are you okay?" Jacqueline asked, coming up behind her.

Lana turned around. "That was amazing."

Jacqueline narrowed her eyes, her eyebrows pulled together. Before she could say anything, Grayson joined them. He pointed to the fountain and began walking. Lana followed, using the silence to collect her thoughts, to embrace the newfound magic within her. Could she do it again? How cold would it get? How far would it go? Her thoughts invigorated her and her whole body tingled, as if electrified.

"I don't think anyone saw," Jacqueline said, turning to Lana and offering her a weak smile.

"That's good," Grayson said, his eyes trained in front of him.

All of the excitement coursing through Lana wavered. She watched her parents, not quite understanding their concern. Wasn't it a good thing that she was becoming stronger? Isn't that what everyone wanted? How else would she be able to defeat Alderic?

When they were all standing before the fountain, she watched the glittery water flow from the three circular tiers. She was fascinated by the fountain and the mysterious Orbs it housed. Suddenly, an idea popped into her mind.

A low hum echoed in her ears as she watched the water. Could she freeze it? Would she be able to draw the frost out and cover the fountain? The magic within her bubbled up, rising to the surface.

"Princess Lana?"

A young girl was sitting on the edge of the fountain next to an older woman. She hopped off the edge, but the woman took her hand, holding her back. Grant stepped in front of her, and Lana smirked. What did he think a child could do to her?

The woman looked up; her cheeks flushed as she bowed her head. "We didn't mean to bother you."

The little girl looked at Lana, a large smile on her face. "I want to be a princess too. I want to be just like you."

Like the fog disappearing with the early morning sunrise, Lana's mind cleared. She blinked, pulling herself back from the darkness. A strand of hair fell into her face, and she blew it away, exhaling the confusion with it. Jacqueline sensed the change in Lana and stepped closer, her face pale.

The fountain drew her attention again. The splash of water sent a cold chill down her spine as the image of the frost snaking its way to the teacup overtook her. Lana turned back to the little girl and watched her hop from foot to foot, her energy looking for a release.

"You don't want to be just like me," Lana said. "Where's the fun in that? Be yourself. Always."

"We should go," Jacqueline said, looking at the woman and child. "Please excuse us."

The woman stood. She grabbed the girl's hand. When she bowed, the girl did as well, her eyes never leaving Lana's.

"Things aren't always as they seem," Lana added. "A lot of responsibility comes with being a princess."

"Thank you for your time," the woman said.

Lana smiled in response, not sure what else to say. Jacqueline took her hand.

"Where are we going?" Lana asked.

"Inside," Grayson answered, pointing to the middle of the fountain.

Lana turned back to Jacqueline. When she nodded that it was safe, she hoisted herself over the edge and made her way to the door at the base. She let her eyes adjust to the darkness, thankful that she was still dry. Even though she knew the water would pass off of her, a part of her still expected wet clothes. When everyone was inside, Grayson closed the door. They made their way downstairs, following the light from the torches on the wall.

Lana walked through a large cobweb, thin strands sticking to her face. She let out a small scream of surprise and stumbled. Her hands landed on the cold, hard wall. As they slid down the rough surface, her skin burned.

"Where are we going?" she asked, her voice low, laced with frustration.

"A land called Lenak," Grayson answered, looking back at her. "We won't stay long."

Once Lana reached the bottom of the stairs, she saw the Orbs. The stone room that housed the portals was lit with numerous torches, even though they didn't need their light to see the Orbs of Telorian. They floated in midair and had their own specific hue, which would light even the darkest room. Lana learned that each hue represented the stability of the dimension it led to. Those with green and blue hues led to stable dimensions, while those with red and black hues led to unstable, chaotic dimensions.

"We want to show you something," Jacqueline added. "It doesn't come around often. We don't want to be late."

Grayson stepped up to an orb with an orange hue. Lana frowned, surprised they weren't going to one of the green or blue hued portals. The orb expanded, and Grayson stepped inside. Jacqueline gestured for Lana to pass next. The swirling sea of silver greeted her. It wrapped itself around her, making it difficult to walk. She placed one foot in front of the other, counting her steps in an effort to maintain her focus. She didn't want to get lost between worlds.

When she finally stepped out of the portal she was greeted by darkness. The night sky welcomed them. A cool breeze blew the hair off her face as she studied her surroundings. They were in a large barren field. The air was heavy, making it difficult to breathe.

"Oh good, just in time," Jacqueline said, stepping out of the portal. "I was worried we were going to be too late."

A faint light lit up the horizon, the sun slowly waking from its slumber. Lana put her hands on her hips and searched, looking for something, anything out of the ordinary, the reason for their visit.

"Sit with me," Jacqueline called.

Lana turned and saw her on the ground, her hands clasped in her lap. Grayson sat next to her, while Grant and the soldiers scanned their surroundings. She sat next to Jacqueline, crossing her legs underneath her. Rays of orange, red, and yellow slowly lit up the horizon, pushing the darkness away. She watched the sky, wondering why they were there. What was so special about a sunrise?

At the look of confusion on Lana's face, Grayson said. "There hasn't been a sunrise here in almost a year. Well, what we would call a year."

Lana looked out at the horizon. The faint rays of light intensified. She looked away. Jacqueline and Grayson were looking at each other, sharing a secret she wasn't privy to. Grant had his back to the light, his face trained on the portal, ready to defend in case anyone else joined them. From the looks of it, she didn't think that would happen. This land was deserted, and now she knew why. Who would want to live in a land where the sun didn't rise for almost a year?

"It's a beautiful reminder that the darkness doesn't last forever," Jacqueline said, turning to Lana. "The light's always there, in the background."

The light became so bright Lana had to shield her eyes again. The cold was replaced by the sun's warm embrace. She spread her legs out in front of her, surprised at how fast the light had chased away the dark. The sun was already high in the sky, the once cold, dark landscape now lit up, revealing cracked, dry dirt. A few withered green stalks dotted the landscape. How had they survived almost a year with no sunlight, only perpetual darkness?

"Maybe we should go to Sirmion," Jacqueline said. "To talk to King Simon. We can try again."

Lana shook her head, remembering their disastrous trip. They had only made it to Port Morgan before they were attacked by rebels.

"What's the point?" she sighed.

Jacqueline's lips sank into a small frown. Lana leaned back, soaking in the warm sun. She closed her eyes, and images of the frozen teacup replaced the bright warm light. The dark magic scared her; the demons scared her.

While it was nice to leave Bridian, if only for a short time, it didn't have the desired effect Jacqueline and Grayson had hoped for. Lana thought of how easy it had been for the darkness to overtake her. It had been so subtle; she hadn't even noticed the change. It would only be a matter of time before what little light inside her was extinguished forever.

**4**

---

# MEDORA

Lana lay awake for hours. She hadn't been able to sleep. Her legs began to cramp, and she stretched. Her muscles ached, as if she had spent the last few days in strenuous physical activity. Could it be a side effect of the magic? Everything bad in her life stemmed from it, she wouldn't be surprised if it was some sort of reaction.

Not wanting to dwell on the unpleasant thoughts any longer, Lana stood. After getting dressed she made her way to the door. As she passed the mirror above her dresser, she paused. Her reflection stared back at her. She was surprised to see how pale she had become. She turned from the mirror and opened the door. Grant was standing outside, looking at a picture. At the noise, he put the picture into his pocket and looked up.

"Good morning. I trust you slept well."

"I slept fine." The lie rolled off her tongue. She wanted to ask about the picture, but it felt too invasive. "Did you sleep well? Anyone step on you? The floor too hard?"

"Ha-ha. Alcee was here last night, I just relieved him."

"Nice to know they allow you a break every now and then."

Grant stepped back to let her pass. She hadn't made it far when she turned to look at him. "What did you do?"

He didn't answer. His head shifted to the left slightly. When she didn't say anything else, he gestured, as if letting her know to continue.

"About? You have to give me a little more context."

Lana bit her lip. "To be stuck guarding me. What did you do? It must have been bad."

"I didn't do anything," he answered, shrugging. "Why would you think it's a punishment to protect you?"

"Well, it can't be the best job."

Grant smiled. "It's actually one of the highest positions in the army. It's not a punishment, but an honor."

The answer surprised her. "Really? It just seems so boring."

"It's far from boring." He chuckled. "Now, you're going to be late to lessons. You missed breakfast, again."

"It's fine." Lana waved him off. "I'm not hungry."

Lana wasn't even lying. She really wasn't hungry. As she walked, she spun her ring around her finger. The halls were quiet, and their footsteps echoed. When she stepped into the library, she was surprised to see her classmates. They usually had lessons upstairs. Maris and Mrs. DeGette were standing near the huge fireplace. A hand shot in the air, frantically waving to her. Trevor smiled wide, and Lana made her way to him.

"I was hoping to see you today," he said.

Marnie waved to someone at the door. Lana followed the wave and saw Kiernan. When he saw Lana, he looked the other way. He made his way to an empty seat, curiously far from Marnie.

Lana turned toward her friend. "I'm so sorry. I haven't been a very good friend."

Trevor shook his head. "I know you're going through a lot."

Lana looked away from him. They sat in silence a moment

longer, so many questions on the verge of spilling out. *Where do you think your mom is? Have you talked to Ava? Do you know they found your dad?*

Instead, she said, "How are you?"

"I'm okay," he answered. "I'm so grateful my leg is healing, but I feel off. Almost like the magic here is clouding my head, making me sick. It's uncomfortable."

Lana brushed a stray piece of hair out of her face. She didn't understand, but then again, the black magic had always been inside her. It didn't have the same effect.

"At least it's not black magic. Or the demons."

Trevor shifted again. "I didn't mean anything by it. I know you're dealing with a lot too."

Lana sighed. She hadn't meant to make him feel bad. It just came out. It felt like no matter what she did, what she said, it was always wrong. Magic was magic. Trevor wasn't used to it. As his friend, he had only been looking for understanding.

"I know it's hard." Lana took his hand, squeezing it reassuringly. "If you need to talk, I'm here for you."

He nodded. Lana watched him for a moment longer. If she focused on him long enough, just him, it almost felt as if she was back in Mt. Sinclair. Almost as if she was a normal teenager again, waiting for class to begin at Mt. Sinclair High School.

Terris ran into the room. He looked just as surprised to see everyone in the main library. He made his way to an empty seat near Deliah.

"Nice of you to join us," Ivan called out. "Better late than never."

Maris clapped her hands together once. "As you can see, we've changed our lesson plan. Instead of us giving a history lecture, you will."

"Next week, you will give a short presentation," Mrs. DeGette added. "You'll each be assigned a major city of Telorian. Research the history of your city, the culture, formation, anything you find interesting."

There were a few quiet groans. Lana twirled her pencil in her hands, remembering her time in Mt. Sinclair.

"Isn't it your job to teach us?" Ivan asked.

Mrs. DeGette cleared her throat loudly. "We are teaching you. Research is an important skill to learn. Who can tell me why?"

Everyone was silent. After a moment, when no one ventured a guess, Mrs. DeGette looked around the room. Her eyes danced across those before her, looking for a volunteer.

"Lana," she said. "Would you like to answer?"

Every eye turned toward her, waiting to see how she would respond. Lana shifted in her seat uncomfortably. She didn't want to be the center of attention. She didn't like being put on the spot, especially when she wasn't the one challenging the assignment. Her breath caught in her throat, and she didn't think she could answer coherently even if she wanted to.

"I, uh," she mumbled, stumbling over the words flying at her.

She heard a few snickers. She didn't know what was wrong with her. She narrowed her eyes at Mrs. DeGette, willing her to move along to someone else.

Mrs. DeGette smiled. "What about you, Carter?"

Lana stiffened. It worked. Her cheeks burned, a marker of her embarrassment.

"To make sure what we're saying, or writing, is correct?" Carter answered in the form of a question.

Mrs. DeGette nodded. "Very good. Yes, it is a means to disprove lies and support the truth. It also allows us an opportunity to learn more about people, or places."

"That's why we'll be spending some time doing some research of our own," Maris added.

This brought more grumbling. Lana sank into her seat, trying to disappear. She didn't want to be called on again.

Maris picked up a large teal bowl. "Who would like to pick first?"

Deliah's arm shot up. She was practically jumping in her chair. "Me! Me!"

When Maris was before Deliah, she held out the bowl. Deliah eagerly reached inside. A moment later, she withdrew her hand and unwrapped the cream paper.

"Bridian!" she said loudly. "This will be easy."

"That's not fair," Dominic called. "We all know about Bridian."

"There's always something new to learn," Maris said, making her way to him. "Why don't you go next?"

Dominic sighed but reached inside the bowl. When he withdrew his hand he grumbled, "Imnar."

Maris walked around the room. Terris pulled Sirmion, Carter pulled Altaris, Marnie pulled Arleyth, Nick pulled Rochelle, and Randy pulled Ganyon Falls. When it was his turn, Kiernan reached into the bowl.

"There aren't many left," he said, withdrawing a paper. "Port Morgan!"

Maris moved to Lana, bypassing Trevor. "Your turn, Lana. Trevor, you're exempt from this assignment. We hope you'll be going home soon and just want you to learn."

Lana quickly reached into the bowl, more than aware that all eyes were on her. She wrapped her fingers around the last piece of paper. When she unfolded it, her breath lodged in her throat. She read the letters again, hoping it had been a mistake.

*Medora.*

This couldn't be right. Of all the cities, how had she pulled Medora? The one place she never wanted to think about again.

"I have Medora," she said, her voice cracking.

"All right," Maris said. "You all have your assignments. Our remaining time will be devoted to research. You should be able to find everything you need in these books," she added, gesturing to the shelves.

As her classmates stood, Lana stared at the paper before her. She thought about asking for a new topic, anything had to be better than Medora. Terris ran to her.

"You have Medora?"

Lana held up her paper. "What are the odds?"

"One in nine," Trevor answered, a playful smile on his face.

Lana shot him a look. She wasn't in the mood for jokes.

"This could be a good thing," Terris said. "Maybe you'll learn something useful."

Lana narrowed her eyes at her friend. "I don't have time for this. What I should be researching is how to talk to Amos. How to get these monsters out of me."

"King Mathias released the demons before," Terris whispered. "Any information you can find on him, or the Revatto, may be helpful."

Lana knew he was right. If she had to research Medora, she may as well spend the time looking for anything that could help her. As Terris made his way to a bookshelf, Lana thought about Trevor. What would he do while everyone was researching their paper? Maybe he could help her?

"Trevor," Mrs. DeGette said, joining them. "You'll be working with me today."

"Lana," Maris called. "Do you need help?"

Lana bit her lip. She stood, making her way to Maris.

"Are you okay with Medora?" her instructor asked when they were alone. "We can give you something else."

Now was her chance. An opportunity to change her assignment so she wouldn't have to think about Medora again. But she knew Terris was right. Maybe she could find something useful.

Against her better judgment, she said, "It's fine."

Maris nodded. "Follow me, I'll show you where the books you'll want to focus on are."

Lana followed her past the huge fireplace, into a maze of shelves. Most of her classmates were already spread out, beginning their research. When they reached the back of the library, Maris turned left, stopping at a large shelf filled with dusty leather-bound books.

"This is where you'll want to focus," Maris said. "We actually have a lot of information on Medora."

Lana inhaled deeply, trying to clear the fog that had overtaken her. Maris ran her hand along the row of books on the top shelf, stopping at a large green volume. She slowly removed it and tiny particles of dust flew around them.

"Start here." Maris handed the book to her. "You'll find a lot of Medora's history in this. It was written by Vari Thornton. She was a well-known historian who worked for the Medoran Royal Family. There are even a few maps."

Lana took the book. As the dust settled around them, she sneezed. Maris turned back to the shelf, ignoring her sneeze.

"Bless you," Lana muttered when her instructor didn't say anything.

Maris turned to Lana; her eyebrows pulled together. "What did you say?"

"I sneezed," Lana answered. "When you didn't say bless you, I did."

Maris chuckled. "That's a custom we aren't familiar with. Why would I need to bless you?"

Lana shrugged. She really wasn't sure. It was habit.

Maris turned back to the shelf, removing a small leather-bound book tied with a thin brown cord. "You've heard of the Revatto?" When Lana nodded, she continued. "This is Aldo Linwood's journal. He was a member of the Revatto. This journal was found by your great-great-great grandfather, King Nacaro."

"I think this is a good start, right?" Lana asked, wondering how long it would take to look through both books.

Maris nodded. "Let me know if you need any help."

Out of the corner of her eye, Lana saw a table. She made her way to the nearest chair and sat. When she was comfortable, she picked up the bigger book, moving the journal to the side. Grant moved to the wall, leaning against it. She turned to him.

"I don't suppose you want to help me?"

"Not a chance," he replied.

Lana exhaled loudly. She read the title of the book before her. *Medora: A History* was written in red ink. She placed the book back on the table in front of her, opening the cover. She placed her hands on her lap and studied the picture before her. Spanning both pages was a map of Medora. The first thing she noticed were the caves at the bottom left. She balled her hands into fists, pushing aside the memories. A long blue line, depicting a river, caught her attention. She closed her eyes and remembered jumping from the mouth of the cave into the water below. Her hands involuntarily tightened, as if clinging to Terris as they fell. She opened her eyes, not wanting to relive any more of the memory.

She focused on the map again, her eyes following the river to a castle near the middle of the page. A few smaller bodies of water were near the castle. At the top right was a large mausoleum, drawn with such detail she immediately knew what it was. A grove of trees was clustered near the bottom right and at the top left were a few mountains.

Deliah's loud laughter broke her concentration. She looked up but didn't see her cousin, her table fairly hidden in the small alcove. Lana sighed and flipped through the book. As she thumbed through the pages, a picture caught her attention. She pulled the book closer. A hand-drawn sketch of a large mausoleum surrounded by statues took up the majority of the page. She studied the picture, counting thirteen statues, all standing with bent heads, as if looking at the ground. A chill ran through her as she read the caption.

*The Mournal Fields: Sacred burial plot of the Revatto*

Lana studied the drawing again. The statues looked so life-like she almost expected them to look up from the page. She scanned the words, learning that the Revatto were buried in the Mournal Fields. The thirteen statues were the original thirteen.

She looked up and her eyes drifted to the small journal. She pushed the larger book away and reached for the smaller book. The leather string was tied near the spine. She carefully unwrapped it, letting it fall to the table.

When she opened the cover, faded, cream-colored paper greeted her. On the first page, written in small cursive, was a poem. Lana brought the book closer to read.

> *The burden is heavy,*
> *The darkness within,*
> *From this day forward,*
> *Protected in ashes.*

Someone slammed a book on the table and Lana jumped, startled from the sudden noise. Deliah stood next to her. Her arms crossed.

"What happened?" Deliah asked.

Lana's eyes grew wide. "You scared me."

Deliah sighed. "Dominic was taking over our table. I had no room to work."

"I'm sure there are other tables," Lana said.

"Well, I figured it might be nice to spend some time with you," Deliah mumbled before opening her book.

Lana turned away, her cousin's words reminding her to be

kinder. She took a deep breath, hoping to clear her head. Her gaze drifted to the poem again. What was the burden? What was protected in ashes? She quickly turned the page.

*After the death of King Mathias, our great city prospered once more. King Thaddeus seemed to have broken the curse. Crops were bountiful and trade once again commenced. Until the Medoran War.*

*King Nacaro of Bridian attacked. King Thaddeus was killed, and Medora became a territory of Bridian. Not agreeing with the bloodshed, we moved to the caves. We used our gifts to help the Medoran Royals. Now that they're no more, there's no use for us in the city. We have no interest in helping those that usurped us.*

*But we have found a new purpose.*

"Do you think Nick likes me?" Deliah looked up from her book, chewing her lip.

Lana sighed. She knew she wouldn't get anything else done with her cousin at the table. She closed her books.

"I don't know," Lana answered, wrapping the string around the journal. "We're not exactly friends. I need a break. Do you need help?"

Deliah looked back at her book. "No, you seem preoccupied."

Lana picked up her books and stood. If her cousin didn't want help, it was pointless to sit there. She was done with her history lesson for the day. It felt counterproductive to study the past when she didn't even know if she had a future.

**5**

---

# THE INVITATION

Lana clenched her fists, fierce determination surging through her. She stepped into the cold water and her muscles tensed. Ignoring the discomfort, she walked deeper into darkness, following the light of the full moon.

When the water became too deep, she slowly swam to the spot. It was ingrained in her mind. One hundred years could pass, and she would still remember. The wind blew softly, scattering leaves from the nearby trees. Flashes of the fateful night appeared. She saw Gavril moments before he was pulled underwater. He had been caught unaware. They all had been.

Lana reached into her pocket. She wrapped her fingers around the vial, remembering all she had to do for the black magic it contained. A smile spread across her lips and her breath quickened, excitement coursing through her veins, as she withdrew it from her pocket.

Treading the water, she unscrewed the top. Looking at the full moon once more, she tipped the vial, watching the liquid sink. The inky-blank poison snaked deeper into the lake, spreading. A deep laugh escaped her lips.

Lana's eyes flew open. She looked around the dark room,

beads of sweat dripping off her forehead. Her skin burned and she threw the blankets off, letting the cool air wake her from yet another nightmare.

"It was only a dream," she mumbled, standing up.

Lana made her way to her dresser. She ran her hand along the top. When her fingers found the hair tie, she quickly put her hair in a loose bun, cooling her neck. Even though it had only been a dream, it had felt so real. Almost as if she had been there the night Alderic poisoned the Altarians. Almost as if she was the one who had done it.

A shiver passed through her, and she made her way to the window. She looked out, glad that it hadn't been a full moon. She inhaled deeply. She didn't want to go back to sleep.

After getting dressed, Lana made her way to her bed. As the weight of everything hit her, she fell backward, resting her hands on her stomach. It was times like this she missed her cellphone. She missed aimlessly scrolling, disassociating from the pressures of life.

The more she thought of Mt. Sinclair, the angrier she became. She missed her old life. She missed the lie. Her hands tingled and she stretched her fingers, trying to stop the sensation. She sat up and a thin line of frost spread onto her blue daisy quilt. Her mouth dropped as she watched it cover the blanket. She jumped out of bed and the frost dissolved, melting into the covers.

Lana slowly backed away, trying to make sense of what was happening. When her back hit the far wall, near the window, she slid down. She pulled her knees to her chest and placed her head on them. While her hands stopped tingling, she felt off, as if the magic was on the verge of overflow with no way to stop it. She no longer felt like herself.

Her back arched forward, sinking into herself. She wracked her brain, thinking of something to calm her, something to focus on. All that came was the image of the frost, snaking its way onto the teacup at Calyndra's. Could it be connected to the demons? Or was it only another manifestation of the dark magic running through her? She wanted to talk to her parents. Lana stood on shaky legs. She opened her bedroom door, surprised that Grant wasn't there. In his place was a tall woman. Her black hair was braided down her back. Her dark brown eyes lit up when she saw Lana.

"Good morning," she said, bowing.

Lana was so taken aback by the stranger she couldn't think straight. She was used to Grant outside her door, occasionally Alcee. Brief, intrusive thoughts crept into her mind, and she struggled to make sense of them. She searched her memory, trying to piece if she had seen her around the castle before. Was she a rebel? She was wearing the army's cloak. It even had a tiny crest at the left lapel, same as Grant's.

"Where's Grant?" the words finally came.

"He'll be taking over shortly," the woman answered politely. "My name is Kaz, short for Kazrine. I'll be taking over a few shifts, mostly during the night. I hope that's okay?"

Lana nodded quickly, hoping the woman hadn't taken offense to her question. Kaz smiled.

"I'm sorry," Lana said. "I didn't mean to be rude."

"Not at all," she said, her voice firm. "Your safety is important. Question everyone."

Lana pushed a strand of unruly hair behind her ear. "I want to see my parents."

Kaz snapped her head to the right, her hand on the sword at her waist. Lana heard footsteps and looked up to see another soldier walking toward them. He bowed his head when he saw her. The soldier cleared his throat and Kaz relaxed her stance.

"King Ramos requested to speak to you," he said, looking at Lana.

"Where is he?" she asked. "In his office?"

The soldier nodded. "Yes."

Lana frowned. "Is everything all right?"

The soldier quickly shrugged. "He asked that I bring you to his office. He just received a message from the Council."

"Maybe they changed their mind?" Lana said, the words pouring out.

With a renewed sense of purpose, she ran down the hall. She heard Kaz and the soldier behind her, trying to catch up. A surge of energy propelled her as the adrenaline coursed through her body. This was what she had been waiting for. They were going to let her talk to Amos. She just knew it.

When they were on the first floor, Lana made a beeline to her uncle's office. People were milling about the foyer, waiting for the dining hall doors to open for breakfast. She hadn't even stopped to see if her parents were there.

As soon as she turned the corner, the soldier's standing guard bowed their heads before opening the doors. Grant was among them. Lana ran into the room. Ramos was standing near a window, his hands behind his back.

"Did they change their mind?" Lana asked, trying to catch her breath. "The Council, did they approve our request?"

"No," Ramos answered, his tone flat.

Lana sighed loudly. "I don't understand. He said you received a message from the Council."

Ramos turned from the window. "I did. It was an invitation to the Council Ball...for you. They want to meet you."

"A ball?" Lana asked, her hands falling to her sides. "A party? They invited me to a party?"

Her uncle nodded. He walked to his desk, running his hands along the top before stopping at a thick cream envelope. He picked it up.

"This doesn't make sense." Lana stumbled over her words. "Everything is falling apart. Alderic is still out there. The demons are inside me. They denied our request to talk to Amos...and now they're inviting me to a party?"

"It's more than a party," he said, stepping away from his desk, closer to her, the envelope still in his hands. "This year, the Council Ball falls on the anniversary of the Council's formation three hundred years ago. It's a show of support."

"I don't care what it is," Lana said, her face flushed. "I don't want to meet them unless they'll help me talk to Amos."

Ramos took another step closer. He held out his hands, offering her the envelope. Lana shook her head. She had no interest in reading it. She crossed her arms over her chest.

"I'm not going."

Ramos sighed. He tapped the envelope in his hands and walked back to the desk.

"It's not that easy."

The fire inside Lana burned. She was tired of everyone telling her what to do. She was tired of having no control over her own life. She didn't want to go to the Council Ball. Did they really think she was in the mood to party?

She took a deep breath. "What do you mean it's not that easy?"

"This is a test, Lana. No doubt Johan told them what happened. They want to meet you. They want to see if you're a threat."

"If I fail their test, they'll send me to the Yards?"

Ramos looked away. He didn't have to answer. She already knew. They were looking for an excuse to send her away. To lock her up. It was the easiest way to deal with her. She gathered there was no magic in the Yards, otherwise Alderic would have escaped sooner. Even as a siphon, the magic within her would eventually run out. What would that mean for the demons?

"You won't fail." Ramos sighed. "The Ball's in a week. We have time."

"What happens if I don't go?"

"I fear they'll take that as an admission you don't have the proper control," Ramos answered. "They'll draft a summons. If you fail to appear, reapers will be assigned to escort you to them. If it gets that far, the chance that you'll be sent to the Yards vastly increases."

The enormity of the situation hit her. She shook her head, trying to think of a plan. Would she be able to convince the Council that she wasn't a threat? She knew she had to try. The room spun, flashes of color appearing before her. She stepped backward, trying to gather her bearings. Her breathing was frantic as she tried to calm her nerves.

"We have a week," Ramos said, taking her arm, pulling her back. "We have time to prepare. You'll go to the Ball and meet them. Don't give them anything to worry about. It'll be fine."

A fresh batch of tears overtook her. She let them fall, unable to stop them. Her eyes burned and her throat hurt. She couldn't think straight.

Ramos placed his hands on her shoulders. "We'll get through this."

Lana wiped a tear from her eye. How was she going to get through this? She could barely handle life at the castle.

"Will you come with me? Will I have to go by myself?"

"I was invited as well," Ramos answered. "You won't be alone."

Lana looked around the room. Ramos studied her, making sure she was okay. What would she do if she lost control at the Ball? Would she even be able to control her magic? She thought of the frost. She couldn't even control that.

"What about my parents? Terris? I can control the magic with him. Everything just feels easier when he's with me."

"I'll see what I can do," Ramos said.

Lana nodded. She wrapped her cloak tighter around herself. Her stomach fluttered, almost as if the darkness inside her was spreading. She had to control her emotions. She couldn't let them win.

"I need to be alone."

Ramos took her hand, preventing her from leaving. "Lana, don't give into it. The darkness. You're stronger than them. This is a test, one that will soon be behind us."

Lana didn't say anything. What could she say? The room was silent, and she strained her ears, listening for something to distract her. She heard faint talking outside the doors and turned on her heel. When she was in the hall, all talking stopped. Grant and Kaz turned to face her, waiting to see what she would do.

She quickly walked down the hall, into the foyer. She heard her guards behind her but didn't stop to talk. She just wanted to be alone. To sort through everything. She quickly made her way past the dining hall and up the stairs, hoping she wouldn't be seen. At the moment, she didn't even want to see her parents.

Her thoughts were frantic, confusing. A part of her thought everything would be okay, that she had everything under control. She would go to the Council Ball, maybe even convince the Council to let her talk to Amos. The other part wondered if she was really in control—if she was as strong as everyone seemed to think. She hated to admit it, but the thoughts were overwhelming her. Would the Council deem her a threat? Would she spend the rest of her life in the Yards?

Lana was almost to the top of the stairs when she heard familiar voices. She placed her hand on the railing and stopped walking, as if the lack of movement would camouflage her. A moment later, Marnie, Carter, and Randy appeared at the top of the stairs.

"We had all these plans," Marnie said. "He hasn't talked to me at all."

When Marnie saw Lana, she stopped walking. Randy walked into her, caught off guard when she stopped. Marnie stumbled forward and grabbed the railing for support.

"Why'd you stop?" he asked. "You almost fell down the stairs."

"Nothing important," Marnie said, her lips curving into a devious smile, reminding Lana of a cheerleader she knew in Mt. Sinclair.

"Hey, Lana," Carter called, finally noticing her. "Did you eat already?"

Lana shook her head and continued climbing the stairs. "I'm not hungry."

"Anyway," Marnie continued, as they passed each other. "He just stopped talking to me. He was going to take me to The Frosted Square."

"Well, plans change." Carter shrugged. "Maybe you've been reading too much into things."

Lana was almost to the top of the stairs, but Marnie's voice carried, louder than before, and laced with venom. "No, everything was fine until she stepped in."

The air shifted, the energy around her tense. Her stomach coiled into a tight knot and her throat closed. She turned around and watched Marnie make her way down the stairs. Carter and Randy were still behind her.

The darkness within Lana rose, awakened by her emotions. She knew she should just keep walking. She had almost made it to the top of the stairs. She had been so close, but Marnie's comment pushed her over the edge.

Lana didn't even feel bad when Marnie tripped over her feet. She fell forward. The only thing stopping her from tumbling down the remaining steps was that her hand was still on the railing. Carter reached out and grabbed her cloak.

"Watch what you're doing," he said, helping her stand.

"Trip over your feet?" Randy asked, concerned.

The corners of Lana's lips curved upward. She laughed and a surge of energy flowed through her. She ran up the remaining stairs. When she reached the top, she spun around and watched her classmates make their way into the dining hall.

"Are you okay?" Grant asked, his voice low.

Lana turned to look at him. "Never better."

Kaz turned back to watch Marnie, Carter, and Randy enter the dining hall, turning around once they were out of sight. She looked at Grant, the concern showing on both their faces. An energy coursed through Lana. She wasn't sure where it came from but tapped into it, hungry for the power, the sense of control.

As Lana neared her bedroom, she heard a familiar laugh and stopped. It was coming from Trevor's room. What was Deliah doing in his room? She bypassed her own room, her curiosity piqued when she heard Dominic. She slowly stepped up to the door, peeking inside.

"We're going to be late," Terris was saying. "We better go."

Deliah waved her hand dismissively. "It's fine." When she looked up, she saw Lana and her eyes brightened. "There you are! We were looking for you."

Lana stepped into the room. Trevor's room was nice, smaller than hers but cozy. Trevor sat back on the bed and rubbed his injured leg. Though magic had healed the majority of the injury, it had taken a lot out of him.

"I'm not going to the dining hall," Lana began. "I was already down there. Your father wanted to talk to me. Apparently, the Council invited me to their Ball."

The room was silent as her friends processed what she had said. Her cousins looked at each other. Terris narrowed his eyes as if he couldn't quite understand what she had said.

"A ball?" Trevor asked. "Like a party?"

"This can't be good," Dominic said, ignoring Trevor's questions.

Lana took another step into the room, before explaining who the Council was. She also reminded him about the Yards and told him what she knew about the Ball. When she finished, Trevor ran a hand through his hair.

"They don't invite just anyone to the Ball," Terris added. "I've heard they're very exclusive."

"Very," Deliah said. "What are you going to do?"

The question was left hanging in the air. Now that she had a little time to process the invitation, Lana was beginning to feel better. It would be the perfect opportunity to meet the Council, to ask them to reconsider their decision. Even if Ramos didn't agree, she didn't see the harm.

"We're going," Lana said, her confidence growing. "He thinks that it would look bad if I didn't go, almost like it would be an admission that I can't control them, that I'm a danger. I have to say, I've been feeling a little better, stronger even. I think I've got this."

"That's good," Trevor said.

Terris cleared his throat. "Are you sure, Lana? This is dangerous. If the Council has any doubts—"

"What else am I supposed to do?" Lana snapped and his face fell. "I have to go. But I'm going to make the most of it. I'm going to ask them to reconsider. See if they'll let me talk to Amos."

Deliah crossed her arms over her chest. "Does my dad know you're going to ask them to reconsider?"

Lana looked away. Her mind was already made up anyway. There was nothing they could do or say to change it. She looked back at Terris.

"He's going to see if you can come with us," she said, her voice cracking. "Everything's easier with you."

He nodded. Deliah ran to Lana. She wrapped her arms around her. Lana's fingers tingled. She stepped out of the hug but still held her cousin's hands. A current of warmth started at her fingertips and ran through her, up her palms and into her arms. Deliah gasped. She pulled her hands away, but Lana held tight, not wanting to lose the feeling. She was pulling her cousin's energy. Her skin prickled, alight with a life its own.

"What's going on?" Dominic said, stepping closer to his sister. "Deliah, are you okay?"

Deliah's eyes grew big, and she sucked in a deep breath before collapsing to the ground. Dominic ran to his sister. Lana's hands continued to tingle, and she held them up, looking at her palms. Even though nothing looked off, they felt electric. Terris joined Dominic, trying to wake Deliah. The lights flickered and Trevor stood from the bed.

"What did you do to her?" Dominic asked, before turning back to his sister. "Deliah, wake up."

The lights dimmed and Lana looked at her hands again. She didn't know how to answer. Even though she knew what had happened, she didn't want to admit it. She had drained Deliah. She had stolen her magic, her energy. And all it took was a touch.

**6**

---

# A SPARK OF HOPE

Terris ran into the hall, looking for help. Lana couldn't move, her muscles tense. A low ringing echoed in her ears. The room spun and her legs quivered. Grant ran into the room and knelt next to Deliah. She startled but didn't open her eyes.

"She'll be all right," he said a moment later. "Bring her to—"

The ringing in Lana's ears intensified. She couldn't hear anything else. Dominic looked at her, his face pale and his nostrils flaring. The energy in the room became too much and she spun around, making her way to the hall. Terris stood near the door. He made a move to block her before thinking better of it and stepping away.

Before she knew it, Lana found herself in her bedroom. She closed the door behind her and fell to the floor. Her hands flew to her head, trying to stop the ringing. It was so loud she couldn't think clearly.

After what felt like hours, the ringing stopped. Lana opened her eyes, taking a few moments to gather her bearings. She stood and stretched, holding her hands high above her head.

She let them fall to her sides and raised her shoulders, lifting the right to her ear, followed by the left. The movement foreign, her body heavy. She inhaled deeply and made her way to the window. The sun was shining, but that wasn't what caught her attention. Her reflection smiled back at her. She looked radiant. Her skin was glowing, and her lips curved into a small smile.

Deep down, she knew something was wrong. Even her appearance frightened her. She looked different. It wasn't her. The demons had control. She tried to scream, to let Grant know that something was wrong, but nothing came out. Movement in the hall caught her attention and her head snapped toward the closed door.

A thin line of frost extended from her feet. She waved her hand, and the door flew open. Grant jumped, surprised by the noise. Not wanting to be bothered, Lana waved her hand, and he flew against the wall. He fell, his head bouncing off the floor. She stepped over him, the line of frost covering his still body.

Lana slowly made her way down the quiet hall. When she found herself at the stairwell, she placed her right hand on the railing and watched the frost slowly cascade down the steps, covering the staircase completely. She descended, but when she heard people in the dining hall picked up her pace. Excitement washed through her.

Before she had reached the dining hall, the demons released their hold on her. She stepped backward. The sudden return of control jarring her senses. She raised her arms in the air and sighed with relief when they moved, following her command.

Her knees wobbled as she stepped forward, her thoughts racing. She couldn't let them win. What would they make her do? Who would they make her hurt? She ran down the hall, toward her uncle's throne room. She didn't know how long she would be herself and needed his help.

The guards standing outside the throne room looked up,

surprised to see her. Lana picked up her pace, eager to talk to her uncle, when the frost appeared again. The pure white ice came out of her feet. Just as fast as it appeared, it ignited. Bright violet flames devoured everything they came in contact with.

Lana stopped running. The ringing in her ears resumed and she fell to the floor, holding her head in her hands. The guards had left their post and were attempting to extinguish the flames. The door to the throne room opened and Grayson appeared.

"What happened?" he called, making his way past the flames toward her.

The darkness overtook her much quicker this time. It had been so seamless she didn't even notice until it was too late. She blinked, taking in her surroundings. When she stood, she waved her hand and the flames disappeared. Undeterred, Grayson kept walking.

"Lana?" he called, his eyebrows pulled together, creating a deep rivet in his forehead. "Is everything okay?"

The voice that answered wasn't her own. "Perfect."

The hair on Lana's arm prickled and her stomach sank. Her voice was off, deeper than usual. She was a passenger inside her own body. As hard as she tried, she couldn't take back control. Her actions, her voice, weren't hers, although her thoughts were.

"Where's Grant?" he asked, eyes darting down the hall. "Why are you alone?"

Lana fought for control. She wanted to warn him, to tell him what had happened. Instead, she shrugged and continued walking. The two guards stepped in front of her slowly, as if sensing the change, understanding that something was off, and their king may be in danger.

With a wave of the hand, everything around her froze. She walked past the two guards, both silent and still, trapped in the moment. When she was before Grayson, she stopped. His eyes were trained on her. His vacant look haunting.

The need to look away, the sudden urge to walk into the throne room, pulled at her, but she fought to keep her gaze on him. Her stomach churned and rage boiled inside her. She wanted her life back. The unbridled anger raced through her, but it hadn't been enough to shake their hold. Images of both Grayson and Jacqueline played in her head, a living book of memories. She wanted to help him. She wanted to unfreeze him.

Their hold on her wavered. Grayson flinched, his face pale with surprise when he saw her so close. He regained his composure and reached for her hands. Before he could say anything, panic surged through her, wrapping her in its cruel embrace. When she closed her eyes, her legs gave out and she fell to the floor. A cold chill snaked up her spine, the disorientation clouding her. Her ears were heavy, the pressure blocking the noise of the world.

"Hello, Lana," a cold voice said.

She opened her eyes. She was no longer in the hall outside the throne room. She was standing in a dark room.

"Who's there?" she asked, breathing heavily. "Where am I?"

A figure emerged from the shadows and Lana's breath caught in her throat. The man stepped forward, small trails of ice-blue frost leading the way. The stranger studied her, his lips pursed and his eyes bright.

The frost made its way toward her, and she involuntarily stepped back. Shadows danced at the man's feet as the ice circled her, encasing her in its cold perimeter. Her stomach clenched and her eyes swept the room, looking for an escape.

"Lana," the man said, stopping at the edge of the circle. "I'm honored to meet you."

Her heart raced so rapidly she couldn't think straight.

Where was she? Who was the man before her? What was controlling the frost?

"Who are you?" she asked, the words tumbling out of her mouth.

The air crackled around them, electrified. The frost dissolved before her eyes, and she let out the breath she had been holding. For some reason she felt safer away from the confines of the circle. She wrapped her arms across her chest, trying to warm herself.

When the stranger made no move to answer, she said, "I asked you a question."

The man's lips curved into a sharp smile. "Yes. You did."

Silence hung between them. Lana tried to steady her frantic breathing, waiting for his answer. She knew she could stop time, or teleport to safety, but curiosity overtook her. She wanted to know who he was, where she was.

"You won't be able to pronounce my name," the man finally answered. "I'm not from this land."

Lana's eyes narrowed. "Where are you from?"

"It's not important. What's important is that I was called here. We were called here."

He held his hands out, palms up, and more shadows filled the room. Lana shivered as the realization hit her.

"Are you one of them...a demon?"

"I've been called that before," he answered, his voice low. "I'm not a demon in the traditional sense of the word."

The man took another step toward her. The shadows dipped throughout the room, coming closer before slinking away. She turned the words around in her head, trying to make sense of them. *I've been called that before.* What did that mean? Was she dreaming?

"What did you do to me?" Lana asked, remembering her cousin. "What's happening to me? I don't feel right."

"We're getting stronger," he answered. "We want the same thing."

The man took another slow step forward, the frost darting toward Lana. She jumped to the left, away from the line of ice. When she caught her balance, she held her arms out toward the stranger.

"Stop."

"Forgive me," he said. "I've been imprisoned for too long. We only want our freedom back. Surely you can understand that?"

"How did you make me move? You were controlling me, but I was myself...I don't understand what's happening."

"We can only control your movements, your voice. Your thoughts are your own...for now."

Lana's mouth ran dry, and she swallowed. The hair on her arms prickled, as if just now realizing the evil before her. Now she wanted to leave. She didn't care who he was, or what he wanted. The man sensed the change and inhaled deeply. A moment later, the frost burst into flame, surrounding her. The shadows continued to swirl around the room, darting every-which way.

"Until next time," he said, the dark shadows swallowing him.

Lana startled awake. Beads of sweat dripped down her forehead and her heart thudded inside her chest. She opened her mouth and inhaled a lungful of air, trying to steady her nerves. What had just happened?

She sat up, surprised to find that she was in her bedroom. She didn't remember coming back to her room. The gentle tick of the grandfather clock drew her attention and she turned toward it. She watched the pendulum glide between its encasement, lost in thought for only a moment. She wanted to see her parents, she wanted to see Grant. She had to apologize. Even though it hadn't been her, the guilt clung to her.

The more she thought about it, the best place for her was the Yards. She didn't want to hurt those she cared about. She didn't want to chance Alderic somehow releasing the demons from her. Worse, she didn't want to succumb to them.

The dream had frightened her. If it had been real, if they had found a way to talk to her, even in dreams, they were growing stronger. How much longer would she be able to fight them? How much longer could she carry on?

Lana made her way to the door, eager to find her parents. She was scared. She wanted their help. She needed them to give her the answer, to fix it.

When she opened the door, she was surprised to see not only Grant, but her parents. They were sitting on the floor, silent and still. Jacqueline's head popped up as soon as the door opened. She jumped up and ran to her but stopped short when Grayson held her back.

"Grayson." Jacqueline turned on him. "What are you doing?"

He cleared his throat, his eyes trained on Lana. "We shouldn't overwhelm her."

Lana blinked, trying to process everything. Even though he hadn't said it, she knew what he meant. He wasn't really worried about overwhelming her. He was concerned that it wasn't her. He didn't want Jacqueline to get hurt.

Before she could stop them, tears began to fall down her face. She quickly wiped them away and sucked in a deep breath, trying to stop the flood of emotions from overtaking her. Jacqueline threw her arms around her, hugging her tight. A moment later, Grayson joined them.

For a moment, Lana savored the comfort of the hug. She felt like a little girl again, safe in their embrace.

"It's okay," Jacqueline whispered. "We'll figure this out."

Lana nodded even though she didn't believe it. What could they do?

"Can we leave?" Lana's voice cracked. "I just want to go somewhere...away from all of this."

"We are leaving," Jacqueline said, stepping back but still gripping her shoulders. "We're going to Ganyon Falls, until the Council Ball."

Lana's eyes were heavy, and she wiped away another stray tear. Of all the places, why were they going to Ganyon Falls? Grayson sensed her confusion.

"Emeric thinks he may be able to help prepare you to meet the Council," he answered. "Leaving Bridian may be the change you need."

Lana wasn't so sure a change was the answer. Would it only set her off? Would it be the thing that brought her over the edge? Her mouth opened. Her lips parted, but the words didn't come. She couldn't push them out.

Jacqueline's hands flew around her again, wrapping Lana in a tight embrace. Over her mother's shoulder, Grant offered her a small smile, letting her know everything would be okay. She closed her eyes and sank into the hug.

"Is Deliah all right?"

"Yes," Grayson answered simply.

Jacqueline brushed a strand of unruly hair out of Lana's face, her fingers brushing against her daughter's cheek. The hall was quiet, leaving Lana to wonder where everyone was. What day was it? What time was it?

"We're going to stay with you until we leave," Jacqueline said, subtly nodding her head toward Grayson. "We think if you're with people, and distracted, it will be harder for them. We were wrong. I'm so sorry."

Lana stepped back to look at her. Jacqueline quickly wiped a tear from her eye.

"We thought giving you space, leaving you alone, was helping," Grayson said.

Jacqueline nodded. "I think it did more harm than good."

Lana didn't think that was true. She had been with her cousins, Trevor, and Terris when the demons overtook her. But she wanted to be with her parents. She didn't want to be alone. Especially if these might be her last days. Her future was clear. She would either lose herself to the demons or be imprisoned in the Yards. She wanted to spend her remaining time with her family.

"I'm so sorry," Lana said when she caught Grant's attention.

A small shiver passed through her when the image of the frost covering his still body flooded her thoughts. She was relieved he was okay, that the frost hadn't hurt him.

"It wasn't you," he answered, his eyes darting away.

Jacqueline ushered her back into her room. When they were inside, Lana sat on the bed. Jacqueline sat next to her. Lana bit her lips, flinching when her teeth touched the dry, cracked skin. She had wanted to see Violette, one of the healers that lived in the castle. A few weeks ago, she had given Lana a paste to put on her lips that helped with the dryness. She had run out but hadn't made her way down to see her yet.

"Why were you in the hall?" Lana asked, leaning against the headboard. "Why didn't you come in?"

"We wanted you to rest," Grayson answered, his eyes darting to the crystal ball hidden underneath the dresser.

Kiernan had given Lana the crystal ball when they first met. She shuddered at the memory of the visions she had seen in it.

"So," Jacqueline began. "Tell us about lessons. How is your research on Medora coming along?"

Lana frowned. For a moment, she wondered if she heard right. She had far bigger things to worry about. Why was her mother asking about her homework?

Jacqueline's face fell. "Let's keep our minds off everything heavy. If we act like everything's okay, it will be."

Lana looked at Grayson. He didn't move. His face was pale, and he set his palms on his knees.

Lana played along. "Not good. I haven't had a chance to really start."

"How can we help?" Jacqueline asked.

Lana stood and made her way to the pile of books she had taken from the library. She scooped them up, along with her notebook and walked back to the bed. When she sat down, she opened the notebook to a blank page.

"Well," Jacqueline encouraged, her eyes shining with the excitement of a project. "What have you got?"

Lana gestured to the blank page. "Nothing."

Grayson chuckled. Jacqueline turned to face him, her eyes narrowed and her face stern. She turned back to Lana and took a deep breath. Lana bit her lip again, only to immediately regret it when the cracked, dry skin burned. Her eyes drifted to the books, and she remembered the poem.

"Actually, I found this poem. Have you heard of it?" She opened the book and began to read. "The burden is heavy. The darkness within. From this day forward. Protected in ashes."

"That's the Revatto's motto," Grayson answered. "Their charge."

Lana looked down at the book again, rereading the poem. She didn't understand. "What burden? What's protected in ashes?"

"If I remember correctly," Grayson began, "the burden is their duty to protect the Medoran Royals. Protected in ashes literally means it is their sacred duty to protect them at all costs. They make a vow to serve until their death."

Lana ran her hand along the paper, her fingertips gliding across the thick textured page. "How were they picked?"

Jacqueline raised her eyebrows, looking at Grayson, trying to put her thoughts into words. "They were recruited, right?"

He nodded. "Yes. They were selected for their talents. They were usually very gifted healers, psychics, and intuitives. After the war, they moved to the caves."

Lana already knew this. She had read about it in the journal. Visions of the caves of Medora flashed before her. It hadn't been that long since she had been there. Alderic had brought her to him. He was hiding in the caves, the place he had called forth the demons.

"When we were in Medora," Lana said, pulling her cloak tighter across her chest for warmth. "We escaped Alderic and ran into the caves. Rebels were digging, looking for something. Do you think it's connected to the Revatto? They used to live in the caves."

A knock at her door interrupted them. It opened, and Grant looked in. He waved Grayson to him before disappearing back into the hall. Their conversation, and Lana's question, all but forgotten.

"They must be here," Grayson said, looking at Jacqueline. "I'll be back."

Lana closed the book. "Who?"

"Calum and Elijah," he answered. "They came for your birthday."

Her stomach sank. She was excited to see them again but didn't want to think about her birthday. What did it matter? Prior to learning the truth, before returning to Bridian, she had looked forward to it. She had been excited to learn how to drive. Now, there was nothing to look forward to.

"I'll be back," he added, standing from the floor.

Lana watched him leave. Before he could close the door, loud footsteps echoed in the hall.

"Can we see her?" Deliah's voice called.

"Now may not be the best time," Grayson said.

Lana looked at her mother. She wanted to see her cousin. She wanted to see if she was really all right. Jacqueline nodded, seeming to understand her thoughts.

"I want to see her," Lana called out, jumping to her feet. "Let her in."

Deliah ran past Grayson, followed by Dominic and Terris. Lana pushed the books and the notebook away, making room on the bed.

"Trevor will be up," Terris said. "He's with Violette."

Lana's stomach sank again. "Is he okay?"

Terris nodded. "He's fine. She was making him something for the nausea."

Lana looked at Jacqueline. "Can I have a moment with them?"

"I don't—"

"Please," Lana said. "Only a minute."

She wanted to apologize. She couldn't do it in front of Jacqueline. It was too awkward. She just needed a moment alone.

Jacqueline stood. "I'll be in the hall. Door stays open."

Deliah sat on the floor, putting as much distance as she could from Lana. Lana couldn't blame her. She didn't know what else she was capable of.

"I'm really sorry, Deliah," Lana said. "I don't know how it happened."

Deliah waved her hand dismissively. "I'm fine. I know you didn't mean it."

"How are you?" Terris asked, watching her closely, as if he was waiting for her to change before his eyes.

"I'm fine. As fine as I can be."

"That's why we're here," Dominic said excitedly.

"We thought of something," Deliah added, her eyes wide. "Actually, Terris thought of it."

Lana turned toward her friend. He uncrossed his arms and looked toward the open door.

"It's just an idea," he whispered. "Don't get too excited."

"Okay," Lana agreed. "What's the idea?"

Terris looked at the ground. "Well, you siphoned some of Deliah's energy."

Lana's stomach clenched, the guilt eating at her. It shouldn't have happened. Deliah could have been seriously injured. If something had happened to her, she would never forgive herself.

"Maybe it will work in reverse," Terris added.

Lana's eyes met his. She didn't understand. She watched him, waiting for him to continue. Everyone was looking at her, waiting for her to react.

"What do you mean, work in reverse?" she asked. "I don't get it."

"You took Deliah's energy," Dominic said. "Maybe you can transfer yours, your magic, into someone, instead of taking it?"

"And maybe that's how you get rid of the demons," Terris finished.

Lana was silent as she thought. Could it be that simple? She was a siphon; she pulled magic out of the air itself. Maybe it would work in reverse, and she could push both Terris's magic and the demons out of her.

"Try it with me," Terris said. "Try to push the magic into me."

Lana knew she shouldn't. That it wasn't the best idea. They needed to think about it, to determine if it was safe. But her curiosity overwhelmed her. She knew Jacqueline was right outside the door. Maybe she should tell her their plan. Maybe she could help? As soon as the idea flashed through her, she realized Jacqueline would tell her to wait. But it was his magic anyway. She had taken it. Maybe she could give it back, begin to make things right.

She stood before her friend. He held his hand out and she took it. As she wrapped her fingers around his, her skin tingled. She wasn't sure what she was doing and had a fleeting moment of panic. She almost dropped his hand, concerned that she would siphon more of his magic.

"You got this," Terris said, gripping her hand tighter.

Lana looked up at her friend, meeting his eyes and holding his gaze. Terris inhaled loudly as the energy between them intensified. She closed her eyes, imagining his magic being pushed back into him. In her mind's eye, she saw gold sparks flowing from her, down her arms and through her fingertips, into his skin.

The air between them crackled and Lana opened her eyes. A bright spark of light danced above their skin. She looked up, locking eyes with Terris again. When the spark faded, she dropped his arm. She didn't feel any different. Could it have worked? When she had taken from Deliah, she felt reenergized, rejuvenated. She assumed that meant if it had been successful, she would feel the opposite. She felt exactly the same.

"Did it work? How do you feel?"

Terris held his arm, flexing his fingers. "I don't feel any different. But did you see that spark? I think you were close."

"What's going on?" Jacqueline asked, stepping into the room. "Lana, are you okay?"

Lana turned toward the door, smiling at her mother. "I'm fine," she answered, sitting back on the bed.

For the first time in a while, it hadn't been a lie. She was fine. Terris was onto something. She would be able to transfer his magic back to him, with practice. Once she accomplished that, she would figure out how to push the demons out. She wasn't sure where they would go, or if it would be that simple but it was something. The spark of light was the sign she needed, and she clung to it.

# 7

# LANA'S BIRTHDAY

Lana threw the blankets to the side and faced the window. Another night of tossing and turning. Next to her, Jacqueline mumbled in her sleep. Grayson had awoken early to spend time with his brothers. While she had been happy to have her mother with her, she wanted to be alone to sort through her jumbled thoughts.

Usually, her birthdays were filled with celebration, but this year was different. This year, there was nothing to celebrate. When she used to think about her sixteenth birthday, she would be filled with hope, excited for the future. Alderic had stolen that from her.

She stood and quickly made her way to the window. As she looked out at the city she was destined to rule, her stomach sank. The sun began its ascent and rays of amber lit up the dark sky. She opened the window, sliding the glass, and inhaling the crisp morning air.

"What are you looking at?" Jacqueline asked, still groggy.

Lana turned from the window. "I was just watching the sun rise."

Jacqueline yawned before sitting up. "Happy birthday. How does it feel to be sixteen?"

Lana shrugged. She could honestly say she felt the same. She didn't feel any different than the day before.

"I'm really proud of you," Jacqueline said, stepping out of bed and joining her at the window. "Grayson and I are both really proud of the woman you're becoming."

Lana wrapped her arms around her mother. "I love you."

Jacqueline wiped a tear from her eye. "I love you more. I'm going to get ready. Remember, you have the dress fitting this morning."

Lana exhaled loudly. They would be leaving for Ganyon Falls tomorrow. The Council Ball was in a week. Although she needed something to wear, she didn't want another reminder of the occasion, especially on her birthday.

When she was showered and dressed, she sat on her bed, crossing her legs underneath her, and drummed her fingers on her knees. Voices carried in the hall, and she ran to the door. Jacqueline was helping a young woman steer a rack of gowns. Lana's face fell at the thought of having to try them on. Grant chuckled before saying, "Happy birthday."

"Thanks," she mumbled.

The woman steered the cart through the door and Lana stepped out of the way. The wheels squeaked as it crossed the threshold, adding to her annoyance. The woman immediately began removing gowns, draping them over her arm. Jacqueline turned to face Lana, waving her over.

"That's my cue," Lana mumbled under her breath.

Grant smiled. "Good luck."

Jacqueline appeared behind Lana and closed the door. "This is Ivy. She'll be helping us."

"It's a pleasure to meet you," the woman said, bowing.

Ivy walked to the other side of the clothes rack and withdrew a long-sleeved sparkly gray ball gown. The bodice was decorated with tiny pearls. She held it out and Jacqueline draped it over her am, approving. Next, Ivy moved to a pale-blue gown, covered in silver sequins that sparkled in the light. Without waiting for Jacqueline's approval, she passed it to her before moving to a red gown with lace tulle.

"Aren't these a little...dressy?" Lana asked.

While the gowns were beautiful, they weren't what she was expecting. Even though it was a ball, she pictured herself in simple attire. She couldn't meet the Council overdressed. She needed to blend in.

"Oh no." Ivy's face paled. "If we had more time, we could have had one custom-made."

"These will do," Jacqueline reassured the woman, glaring at Lana. "It's a ball, Lana. Everyone will be dressed up."

"They're beautiful," Lana said, not wanting to upset Ivy. "I just didn't know that it would be so...fancy."

Ivy's eyes danced between Lana and Jacqueline, as if trying to understand Lana's reluctance. Jacqueline smiled widely before pointing to a shorter navy dress. Ivy tilted her head, studying the dress before removing it and placing it on top of Jacqueline's pile.

"We'll start with these," Ivy said, her eyes snapping back to the cart, her eyebrows pulled together as if silently debating the merits of each remaining dress.

Jacqueline dropped the gowns on the bed. Lana picked up the red gown, running her hand along the tulle. She quickly changed and turned to the mirror above her dresser, studying her reflection. The dress fit perfectly, but it didn't feel right. It didn't feel like her.

"You look beautiful," Jacqueline said. "But you have that face. I know you don't like it."

"I like it," Lana quickly said, not wanting to upset Ivy. "But I don't know, it just doesn't feel like me."

Ivy waved her hand in a circle, signaling that she should try on the next. Lana stepped into the pale-blue dress, but it was too big.

"We can take that in," Ivy said.

"That's okay," Lana said. "I don't think this is the one either."

Even though the dress would work if it was taken in, she didn't like it. The pale-blue color reminded her of the frost. She didn't need a constant reminder of that. She tossed the dress back to Jacqueline and picked up the sparkly gray gown, running her hand along a section of pearls.

"That's my favorite," Jacqueline said. "It's the same color as your cloak. Your mother's cloak."

Lana looked up from the gown. "You're my mother."

Jacqueline smiled. "Kalinia's cloak."

As soon as Lana stepped into the gown, she knew it was the one. It fit perfect. The fact that it was same color as her cloak was an added bonus.

"This is it," she whispered. "I love it."

Ivy tilted her head. She walked around Lana, studying the fit. When she was satisfied, she looked up.

"It doesn't even need any alterations," she said. "It's perfect."

"You look beautiful, Lana," Jacqueline said.

Lana looked in the mirror one last time. What would she do with her hair? What jewelry would she wear? She wanted to make a good first impression. She wanted to feel confident, and comfortable.

"We'll have it sent to Ganyon Falls," Ivy said. "It can't get wrinkled."

"Thank you," Jacqueline said. "Lana, try the navy dress on. I was thinking you can wear it today, for your birthday."

Lana tried to gauge if she was serious. She had no plans for the day. Other than packing for Ganyon Falls. Why would she need to wear a dress?

"We're going out," Jacqueline said, helping Ivy pack up the gowns. "A new dress may be nice."

Lana didn't feel like arguing. She wasn't sure why Jacqueline wanted her to have a dress for her birthday but if she wanted her to try it on, that was the least she could do. She was only trying to help keep her mind off of everything going on in her life. Even though she wasn't a fan of dresses, she would wear it.

"Do you like it?" Jacqueline asked, turning back to Lana when she was dressed.

"Yeah, it's nice," she answered, smoothing the dress down her legs. "Not something I would normally wear, but for my birthday I guess it works."

Ivy looked up. "Do you need shoes?"

Lana shook her head. "I have the perfect shoes."

She made her way to the foot of the bed and pulled out her white sneakers. She bent down to lace them. When she stood, she smiled. "How do I look?"

"Perfect." Jacqueline giggled.

Ivy coughed, trying to hide her disdain. From the look on her face, Lana knew she didn't approve of the sneakers. She made her way to her dresser and ran her hands through her hair, detangling and smoothing her curls.

"I'll send shoes for the Ball," Ivy said curtly, guiding the cart to the door. "Happy birthday, Princess Lana."

Jacqueline opened the door, and Ivy left, pushing the rack. The wheels squeaked as it rolled down the hall.

"How long do I have to wear the dress?"

"Not long," Jaqueline answered, looking at the clock. "We're running late. Grayson is waiting for us."

Lana ran her hands along the fabric again. Her stomach rumbled, and her throat was dry, alerting her that Ivy had been with them longer than she thought.

"When are we going to lunch? I think we missed breakfast."

"We did," Jacqueline answered matter-of-factly. "We're going to Calyndra's for brunch."

Lana shifted on her feet. The last time they had been to Calyndra's was the first time the frost appeared. She shuddered at the memory, the thin line of ice making its way to her cup, devouring it.

"We won't stay long," Jacqueline added, noticing her apprehension.

Lana's throat closed when she realized what Jacqueline was doing. She was worried their time was almost over. She feared the Council would send her to the Yards. She was trying to give her one last normal birthday.

Jacqueline took Lana's hands in her own. "We don't have to go. Do you want to stay? I can have something brought up from the kitchen for you."

Lana shook her head. "No, I want to go. You're right, the busier I am, the better I feel. Almost like everything's normal."

Jacqueline squeezed her hands encouragingly. Lana was willing to try. She wanted one last birthday. She could do this. Even though there were a lot of people at Calyndra's, she hadn't known them. She had been distracted, caught up in her own worries.

Lana followed Jacqueline downstairs. She was surprised at how quiet it was. Grayson was near the dining hall, looking out the window with his back toward them. He turned around when he heard them coming down the stairs.

"You look beautiful," he said. "You both do," he added, looking at Jacqueline.

Lana's cheeks flushed. "Thank you."

"Did you find something for the Ball?" he asked.

"I did."

He smiled before handing her a small cream-colored box. "Happy birthday."

Lana turned the box in her hand. "You didn't have to get me anything."

"Of course, we did," Jacqueline said, putting her arm around Grayson's. "Sorry, there's no wrapping paper. It isn't customary to wrap gifts in Bridian."

Lana opened the box. A silver charm bracelet greeted her. She lifted it to look at the heart-shaped charm and saw a tiny clasp on the side. Jacqueline took the empty box.

"It's a locket," she said. "Open it."

A gasp escaped her lips. Inside were two small pictures. The picture on the right was of Lana, Jacqueline, and Grayson taken in Mt. Sinclair. On the left was a woman with an infectious smile. Kalinia. Lana felt the harsh sting of tears and looked away, not wanting to cry.

"Do you like it?" Jacqueline asked, her voice cracking. "We can get you something else."

Lana tightened her hands around it. "I love it. Now you'll be with me, wherever I go." She closed the locket and raised her right arm. "Can you put it on?"

Jacqueline clasped the bracelet on Lana's wrist and stepped back. They stood in silence a moment longer and Lana was grateful for the quiet time with her family. Even though Grant was with them, standing near the doors, it felt almost normal, as if it was just another day in Mt. Sinclair.

"Are you ready?" Grayson asked.

"Yes," Lana said eagerly. "I'm hungry."

Grant led them outside. It was a beautiful day in Bridian, and she was glad she hadn't worn a cloak. The sun warmed her skin and her spirits lifted.

When they reached the back alley near Calyndra's, Grant allowed Grayson to pass first. He climbed the stairs and opened the door, disappearing into the shop. Jacqueline was right behind him. Lana followed, surprised to see Carter pass by the door. When he saw her, he waved.

As her eyes adjusted to the change in light, Lana followed Grant. A familiar laugh caught her attention and she looked up to see Deliah sitting at the bar, laughing with Nick. To his right was Dominic. Randy stepped out from behind a shelf.

"Happy birthday," he said.

Deliah looked up when she heard him. She called out, "Happy birthday!"

Everyone in the shop turned toward Lana. Her face flushed from all the attention. She looked at her parents, knowing this was their doing, when another voice made her pause. Her eyes darted across the shop, past Elijah, Calum, and her classmates, finally stopping on the girl sitting next to Trevor. Ava smiled. At first, Lana didn't understand. Her two worlds collided, yet again, and she tried to process it. Why was Ava in Bridian?

Her hands flew to her mouth. She looked at her parents again, tears filling her eyes. They had planned this. They did this for her. How had they convinced Ava's parents to let her come? Did they tell them the truth? Just as fast as they came, the questions escaped her. She ran to her friend, dodging some of her younger classmates.

"What are you doing here?" Lana asked, hugging her friend tightly.

Ava rolled her eyes. "Like I would miss your sixteenth birthday."

"You planned this?" Lana turned to her parents. When they nodded, she continued, "How long have you been working on this?" Without waiting for an answer, she turned back to Ava. "How did you get here? Do your parents know? Where do they think you are?"

The questions flew out, her brain working in overdrive, trying to make sense of it. Ava giggled, placing her hand on Trevor's shoulder before leaning closer to him. "She's been gone too long if she thinks my parents would let me come here."

Lana turned to her parents. "How? What did you do?"

"Well, they think you moved to Florida," Ava rushed to explain, another giggle escaping her lips. "Your parents asked them if I could spend the weekend with you for your birthday. It took some convincing from your mom. They even bought flight tickets to make it seem more realistic."

Lana smiled at them in gratitude, one hand on her chest, the charm bracelet dangling from her wrist. Ava sat next to Trevor, and Gareth appeared with another chair for Lana. Someone placed a Choclochino in front of her.

"There's more," Grayson said. "We got you pizza from Charley's."

Lana's mouth began to water. Charley's Pizzeria was her favorite place to get pizza in Mt. Sinclair.

"And chocolate cake for dessert," Jacqueline added.

Lana looked around the room again, trying to process it all. She couldn't believe her parents did all this for her. When had they managed to talk to Ava's parents, let alone bring her to Bridian? How did they have time to plan it all? She remembered Grayson's conversation with Gareth. He must have been discussing the party with him.

"So, what's it like living with Nick?" Ava asked, her green eyes darting from Trevor to Lana.

"He's been really nice," Trevor said. "It's like talking to a different person."

Ava's eyebrows pulled together. "Seriously?"

"He has been better," Lana reluctantly agreed.

Ava placed her hand on Lana's. "I heard what happened… with the Crystal. Are you okay?"

Grayson placed a slice of pepperoni pizza in front of Lana. She was grateful for the distraction and picked it up. Ava exchanged a worried look with Trevor. Her long black hair hid her face as she sipped her drink.

"This is really good," Ava said, taking another sip of her Choclochino.

"How long are you here for?" Lana asked, trying to change the subject.

"Your parents are bringing me home tomorrow night. I have to say, life's pretty boring without you two."

"I'll be back," Trevor said, leaning into his chair. "As soon as my mom comes home."

Ava took Trevor's hand and squeezed it. "I go by your house every night. As soon as she's back, I'll tell her where you are."

Trevor stood. "I need a few minutes."

Lana slid her chair back, ready to follow. Ava shook her head. Trevor made his way to the window overlooking Bridian Square.

"Don't you think we should go to him," Lana asked. "I haven't been a very good friend lately."

"No one blames you, Lana," Ava said, moving to Trevor's chair so she was closer. "You're going through a lot too. We'll give him a minute alone."

For a moment, Lana wondered how their lives had fallen so off course. She took a bite of her pizza and turned to watch Trevor, surprised to see Nick talking to him.

"I never would have thought they would be friendly," Ava said. "A lot has changed. I feel like we aren't even the same people."

A laugh escaped Lana's lips. She couldn't agree more. She would give anything to go back to the fifteen-year-old girl from Mt. Sinclair.

"I'm really glad you're here."

"I am too. By the way, who is that and why does he keep looking over here?"

Lana turned to see who she was talking about. Kiernan was standing across the room, talking to Randy and Carter. When he saw her looking at him, he waved.

"That's Kiernan," Lana said, looking away quickly.

"He's cute," Ava said, tossing her hair over her shoulder. "Oh, you'll never guess who Laurie Huntington is dating now."

Lana watched as Nick continued to talk to Trevor. "What happened to Bill Polanski?"

Ava giggled. "That didn't last long. Hottie's coming over here."

"Bill?" Lana asked, confused. "What do you mean he's coming over here?"

"Not Bill," she whispered.

Lana followed Ava's gaze. Kiernan was walking toward their table. Seeing him made her stomach flip-flop and she reached for her drink, hoping to steady her nerves. As she drank, her eyes darted around the shop again, looking for Marnie. She hadn't seen her, or Ivan, and wondered if they were together, plotting her demise.

"Hi," Kiernan said, sitting next to Lana. "Happy birthday."

"Thank you."

She wanted to work things out with Kiernan. She hoped they could at least be friendly. Their last encounter turned in her mind. She wanted to apologize but didn't know how to bring it up.

Ava sensed the tension and stood from her chair. "I should check on Trevor."

"That's a good idea," Lana said, standing up to join her.

"I've got it," Ava said, gently pushing Lana back into her seat. "Talk to him," she whispered.

Ava walked away. Kiernan clasped his hands in front of him. An awkward silence fell over them. They were the only ones at the table, everyone else was at the bar or perusing the shop's merchandise.

"I was hoping to talk to you," Kiernan began.

"Actually, I wanted to talk to you too," Lana said, crossing her legs underneath the table.

"Really?" he asked.

Lana swallowed. "I haven't been very nice to you. I guess it's been easier to shut everyone out."

Her cheeks flushed. What was she doing? Why did she tell him that? In their silence, an awkward energy fell over them. She was still embarrassed and didn't even know if she could trust him. But that didn't excuse her from shutting him out.

He cleared his throat. "I know."

Lana bit her lip. Even though everyone was being so understanding, it wasn't right. It had been a mistake to close everyone out of her life. It wasn't helping anything.

"You could have just told me," she added. "When you introduced yourself, you could have just told me that you wanted to get to know me because you were training to be an adviser."

He nodded and a lock of hair fell over his eyes. "I should have. I really am sorry. I do want to get to know you better."

Lana looked away, her eyes darting around the shop at her friends and family. She wasn't used to boys being so direct. In Mt. Sinclair, no one had sought her out. No one wanted to be her friend, apart from Ava and Trevor.

"Do you think we can start over?"

Lana looked back at him. His eyes met hers and her stomach fluttered, halting her breath for a moment. She wanted to start over. Pretend that the miscommunication had never happened.

"That would be nice."

He smiled. "I heard you're going to the Council Ball. I am too. All of the advisers, and advisers in training were invited."

This was news to Lana. She wiggled in her chair, trying to get comfortable. She shouldn't have been surprised. In a way it made sense that he would be invited, that the Council would want to stay on good terms with the advisers.

"I'm really nervous," she said. "Have you met the Council before?"

She looked away, wondering if she revealed too much. She didn't need to push her insecurities on him. He didn't need to know that she was nervous.

"Don't be. They can be intimidating but it will be fine. They're here to help."

Lana bit her lips again. She wanted to believe the Council was here to help but she was beginning to have doubts. It didn't seem as if they wanted to help at all. What have they done to find Alderic? Why wouldn't they let her talk to Amos?

Kiernan reached into his pocket and withdrew a small blue box. He set it on the table and slid it to her. Lana shifted in her chair, wondering what it could be.

"For the Ball," he said nervously. "It's customary for advisers to give small gifts to those they serve before big events."

"You're not an adviser yet," she said.

His gaze dropped. "It's also for your birthday."

Lana studied the box. She slowly reached out and picked it up. She gasped when she opened it. A beautiful silver necklace sat inside.

She looked up at Kiernan, wondering if he made a mistake. When she saw his smile, she knew that it was meant for her and looked at the necklace again. A tiny diamond star was set on a dark blue sapphire, surrounded by diamonds.

"I can't accept this," she said, handing the box to Kiernan.

He frowned. "You don't like it?"

"It's beautiful," she said. "I can't accept it because it's too much. It was probably really expensive."

Kiernan handed her the box again. "It's a gift, Lana. I want you to have it. For the Ball."

"Are you sure?" she asked, silently debating if she should accept the necklace. It was really beautiful, and she would love to wear it.

He nodded. "It looks like a shooting star. It reminds me of you."

Lana looked at the necklace once more. Even the silver chain sparkled. Her stomach sank. She didn't deserve this. She didn't deserve his friendship.

Lana's eyes met his. "Why does it remind you of me?"

He cleared his throat before answering. "They're unexpected."

Lana looked at him curiously, her brow wrinkled in confusion. "I'm unexpected?"

"My feelings for you are," he answered, tearing his gaze from the floor and holding her's.

Lana's heart raced. She briefly wondered if he was joking, if he would start laughing at her for believing he could possibly like her. Then she saw the look on his face, silently pleading for her to say something.

"Thank you."

"I meant what I said, Lana. I like you. I want to continue to get to know you. I know you're going through a lot, and I'll give you your space. But I'm not going anywhere unless you want me to."

Lana swallowed. "What about Marnie?"

He shook his head slightly. "There was never anything with Marnie. She likes me but I like someone else."

Lana didn't know what to say. Her mouth ran dry, and she reached for her drink. She took a sip of her Choclochino, holding the cup to her mouth longer than necessary so she could catch her breath.

"There's something else," he said, his voice cracking. When she turned to him, he continued, "I'm also meeting with the Council. I'm going to ask them to reassign me after my training."

Lana placed the cup back on the table. "I don't understand."

"I'm hoping they'll assign me another kingdom," he answered. "Maybe I'll transfer to another position working with the Council. I can do something else. I don't want there to be any questions about my feelings for you. It's more than the fact you'll be Queen. I genuinely like you, Lana."

She inhaled deeply, trying to hold herself together. Her eyes roamed the room. She said the first thing that came to her. "The Council's in charge of adviser assignments?"

Suddenly, the weight of what he said hit her. He was training to take over for his father as an adviser to Bridian. He was going to transfer to another kingdom or give up the position altogether so there wouldn't be any questions about his motives. He was willing to give it up for her.

He nodded. "One of the main jobs of an adviser is to keep the Council informed of everything that happens in each kingdom."

She thought that was odd but focused on the fact that he was willing to give it all up for her. Even after shutting him out, he still wanted to try. She felt the spark between them and shivered.

"No." Lana placed her hands on the table. "You can't do that."

Kiernan placed his hand on hers. "I want to."

Her hands tingled. Kiernan's touch took her breath away. All other sounds faded, as if they were the only two people in the shop.

"If I get through this, my meeting with the Council, I'd like to hang out more," Lana said, her stomach twisting at her forwardness.

"When you get back," Kiernan said. "Not if. And I would like that."

Lana smiled. She looked at the necklace once more, letting her thoughts wander. She didn't know what was going to happen with her and Kiernan but was excited to find out. That is, if she wasn't sent to the Yards.

8

———

**THE THIRTEEN KEYS**

Lana arched her back, stretching on the grass. Her cheeks burned from the warm sun, and she rolled over, so she was on her stomach. Beside her, Terris had a book open on his lap. Deliah and Dominic had gone inside.

They arrived in Ganyon Falls three days ago. After saying goodbye to Ava and Trevor, Lana packed the last of her bags. Grayson brought Ava to Mt. Sinclair through the mirror near Altaris. Even though Trevor was staying in Bridian, Lana was sad to leave him. She wasn't sure when she would see him again and hoped it would be soon.

Lana had spent her free time thinking about the Council Ball. She was worried that she would do something she shouldn't. Something that they would misconstrue and use against her. She didn't know much about the Council members and wondered if they had already made their decision without even meeting her. Would they help her? Or would she be sent to the Yards? Even though she knew it would probably be for the best, she didn't want to be imprisoned, away from her friends and family.

Terris turned the page of his book. She wished she could

give him his magic back. If she could transfer it to him there would be less inside her. Maybe then it would be easier to control. His eyes ran across the page, and she wondered how he could be so engrossed with so many distractions around him.

"Can we try again?" Lana sat up. "If I can give you some of the magic...your magic, maybe I'll get through the Council Ball."

Terris closed his book and looked at her. "Okay, we can try."

He placed the book on the ground. She looked behind them and found Grant a few yards away, sitting on a bench, his eyes scanning their surroundings. Two more soldiers stood to her right, too preoccupied looking for any threats to pay attention to them. Everyone else was inside with Emeric. Her parents would be out any minute. Jacqueline hardly left her side these days, so they didn't have long.

Lana turned back to Terris. She took his hand. Just being around him calmed her and she focused on that feeling. She imagined the magic flowing through her, into her fingers and through her fingertips. Her skin tingled and heat emanated from her hands. Moments later, the heat was replaced by ice-cold frost.

"Ow." Terris pulled his hand away.

A thin layer of frost covered his hand. He stood, blowing his warm breath on them. It slowly melted. She jumped up and took his hands in hers, ready to try again. She had been close. She felt it.

Terris slid his hands out of hers. "That hurt."

"I'm sorry," she said. "I thought we had it for a minute. Maybe we can try again. After Emeric's lesson?"

Terris raised his eyebrow as if that was the last thing he wanted. Nevertheless, he agreed. Grant was now watching them. Not wanting to draw any more attention she sat back down, stretching her legs in front of her. She wondered what Emeric's lesson would entail tonight. He had spent the past three days telling her everything would be okay. He was convinced that with the right mindset, the right attitude, she could overcome everything. She wasn't so sure but had gone along with it anyway. What else could she do?

A door slammed shut, breaking her from her thoughts. Her hands flew to her chest. Flashbacks of the attack in Port Morgan overtook her. Were the rebels here? Had they found her?

"Dom, that wasn't funny." Deliah marched out of the house. "Why would you do that?"

"It wasn't a big deal," Dominic said.

Lana listened to her cousin's latest argument. Deliah went off on her brother about scaring her. Beside her, Terris groaned and picked up his book, spreading it on his lap again.

"Hey," Deliah called. "Emeric wants to see both of you."

Terris sighed loudly, closing the book again. Lana made her way to her cousins, hoping his lesson would be short.

"I'm going to finish my paper," Deliah said, crossing her arms over her chest. "Are you coming, Dom? You haven't even started yours."

Dominic chortled. "I have more than enough time."

Lana envied her cousins. She wished her only worries involved writing a paper. She followed Terris inside. They found Emeric in the kitchen, talking to Jacqueline and Grayson. She made her way to the table, pulled out a chair, and sat down. She placed her hands on her lap.

Jacqueline stood. She made her way to the sink and turned around. "Would either of you like something to drink?"

"Water," Lana said.

"I'm fine," Terris answered. "Thank you."

Jacqueline placed a glass of water on the table in front of Lana. She sat down just as Ramos entered the room. His eyes were heavy. He walked to the chair at the head of the table and sat.

"How was your day?" he asked, looking at both Lana and Terris.

Lana shrugged. "Fine. For what could potentially be one of my last days of freedom."

The room fell silent. Terris didn't even answer. She knew she shouldn't have said it, that the situation was too serious to joke about. She looked away, waiting for someone else to say something.

"That's not funny," Jacqueline said.

Lana looked up, meeting her gaze. "I know. I'm sorry."

"How are you feeling?" Ramos asked, changing the subject. "Do you feel all right? Have there been any moments you felt like you weren't in control?"

For the past three days, Ramos had asked the same question. "I feel fine," she answered, almost by rote.

"It's been a few days since it happened," Jacqueline said. "Maybe we don't have to worry about it any longer. Maybe you're getting stronger."

"No," Emeric said. "Complacency isn't the answer. That's when cracks form."

As Lana reached for her water, Damarius joined them from the hall. As an adviser to the king, he had been invited to the ball. She still didn't trust him; he had been with the rebels when Alexander had been excavated from his grave. She had seen the look on his face, and it hadn't looked fake.

At the thought of the ball, her stomach dropped. She gulped her water in big sips, trying to settle it. She had two days to prepare. Two days until she met the Council of Elders. Two days to impress thirteen strangers.

"What more do I need to know?" Lana asked, setting the glass back on the table.

"Is there anything you would like to know?" Emeric asked. "Anything that you want more information on?"

Lana pursed her lips, thinking. She had a lot of questions.

Where was the Council Ball being held? Where was the Yards? Who and what gave the Council the power to send someone to the Yards? Why were they even holding a ball in the first place?

"Who are the Council members?" she asked, finally settling on the question she wanted answered the most. "I know there are thirteen members, but who are they? How were they elected?"

"They weren't elected," Emeric answered.

Damarius sat next to Ramos. Lana shifted her gaze from him to Emeric, waiting for him to continue.

"I don't get it," Lana said, "How did they join the Council?"

"That story begins three hundred and seventy-nine years ago," Emeric said, meeting the gaze of everyone at the table. "When a boy found the first portal between dimensions."

Lana found that she was holding her breath. She parted her lips, exhaling slowly. Everyone's attention was on Emeric.

"I heard about this," Terris said, his nose scrunched as if searching for a memory. "It started the hunt."

Emeric nodded. "The young boy was from Noliv. His family was poor. They barely had enough to survive on."

"The portal took him to Arleyth, right?" Grayson said.

Lana remembered Gareth was from Arleyth. The city was known for their silver roses. Emeric clasped his hands on the table in front of him.

"Yes," he answered. "When his family used the portal, they stole food, livestock, jewels, whatever they could find. As the days passed, they returned. If they found something they wanted, they took it by force, murder even."

"Murder," Lana repeated.

He nodded. "It made for an easy escape. When word of the portal spread, a group of scavengers from Noliv began their search for others, calling it the Great Hunt. As more portals were found, a few of the wealthiest families across the dimensions decided to do something. They used the portals to talk to each other, to formulate a plan. They offered rewards for the location of each newly found portal. They cataloged them. With a list, they were able to monitor them."

"Archivists, right?" Lana asked, remembering a lesson about those that monitored the portals between dimensions.

Emeric nodded. "They also hired people to stand guard at the portals. If anyone was caught doing something nefarious, they were imprisoned. During their catalog of portals, a new dimension was found. With only one portal in existence, the uninhabited dimension became the perfect prison."

"The Yards?" Terris asked.

Emeric smiled, pleased that he was following the conversation. "The families pooled their resources to create the Yards. One member from each family became the Council of Elders."

Lana looked around the room, piecing together what she had been told. Her fate depended on thirteen people who were in the position because of something their ancestors did. It didn't seem fair that they had so much control and could send her to the Yards at their whim.

"Wait," she said, her mind working in overdrive. "I don't understand. These thirteen families made themselves the Council. They gave themselves power and no one questioned it? Everyone went along with it?"

"You have to understand how bad it had become," Ramos interjected. "There was no order, no justice. People were using the portals to go into other lands, take what they wanted, sometimes by force, and then escape through the portal never to be seen again. When the thirteen families stepped in, things weren't as scary as the portals were being monitored. When the guilty parties were caught, they were held accountable. That's what everyone supported."

"But how is that fair?" she asked. "The wealthiest families that happened to band together hundreds of years ago have all the power. They, and they alone, determine who goes to the Yards?"

Damarius cleared his throat. "Can't the same be said for kings and queens? The ruling families."

Lana glared at him. Even though what he said was valid, she didn't want to hear it from him. She didn't even know if he was on their side. Jacqueline placed her hand on her shoulder, as if aware of her thoughts.

"They're not out to get you, Lana," Grayson added. "They've done a lot of good. The people they've sent to the Yards deserve it. They don't send innocent people away."

"Well, they didn't acknowledge Alderic's escape from the Yards," she said. "They haven't done anything to find him. They can't be that great."

A heavy silence fell upon the room. Lana reached for her glass and took another long sip of water. Next to her, Terris straightened in his seat. She needed to get through the next two days. Once the Council Ball was past, the threat of being sent to the Yards behind her, she would be able to focus.

"That's the exact attitude you won't be going in with," Grayson said, his voice stern. "Don't put them on the defense as soon as you meet them."

Lana twisted her ring around her finger, trying to keep her emotions in check. She didn't understand how the Council could be good, on their side, if they hadn't even acknowledged Alderic's escape. But now wasn't the time, she was going to play their game. Maybe if she did, she could talk to Amos. Perhaps she could convince them to let her talk to him.

"Where's the Yards?" she asked. "How do you get there?"

Terris looked at Lana out of the corner of his eyes, as if he knew what she was thinking. His lips turned down and he shook his head slowly. Lana nudged him in the side, hoping he would stop.

"We don't know," Ramos answered. "Only the Council does."

Emeric nodded. "It's only accessible with the thirteen keys."

Lana's interest was piqued but she had to play it off as if she didn't really care. If she could find a way into the Yards, she could talk to Amos.

"What are the thirteen keys?"

She reached for the glass of water again, her fingers curling around it. Her charm bracelet hit the side, the sharp tap breaking the silence. She quickly moved her hands back to her lap.

"Each one of the Council members has a key," Ramos added. "They, and only they, can get into the Yards."

Lana couldn't help but wonder if that was the truth. If it was, how had Damon got into the Yards to help Alderic escape? She learned that someone else had been placed in his cell. By the time they realized what had happened, it was too late.

Ramos leaned forward in his chair. He exhaled loudly; his eyes downcast. She knew it wasn't the best time to bring that up, to ask that question.

"Where's the portal?" she asked, settling on the safer question. "You said there was only one in existence. Where is it?"

"I don't know," Emeric answered.

Even though it hadn't felt as if she learned much, she could work with it. At least now she knew she had to look for the keys.

"This is serious, Lana," Ramos said. "Don't do anything you'll regret."

Her uncle's eyes bore into hers. It hadn't been a secret that she regretted going to the Mt. Sinclair Welcome Center. She had been impetuous, and he didn't want her to make the same mistake.

"One thing at a time," Grayson added.

Jacqueline took her hand and squeezed it tight. "The

Council is extremely powerful. They've been around a long time. But they're fair. Don't do anything to make them question your intentions."

"I won't," Lana said, removing her hand from Jacqueline's. "I'm just curious. I want to know everything before I meet them. That's all."

Ramos turned to Terris. "You'll stay with Lana?"

He nodded. He looked at her, offering her a small smile of encouragement before turning back to Ramos.

"I won't leave her side."

"I trust you won't," Ramos said.

"What about us?" Jacqueline asked, her voice tense. "Have you heard anything else about the status of our request?"

Ramos shook his head. "It hasn't been approved. Honestly, I'm amazed they're letting Terris attend."

Lana frowned. She looked at her parents and her heart sank. Jacqueline took her hand again, squeezing it tight. Even though she was thankful to have Terris by her side, she wondered if she would make it without her parents.

As if on cue, a timer buzzed and Emeric stood. He made his way toward the stovetop, stirring the contents of a black pot. He reached over and turned the timer off. The echo continued to ring in her ears, reminding her that her time was soon up.

Lana's fingers tingled and she pulled them out of Jacqueline's tight grip, worried she would drain her. She looked at everyone one last time before standing. She left the kitchen, doing everything in her power to keep the magic, and her emotions, under control.

**9**

---

# THE COUNCIL BALL

Lana inhaled deeply; her already frayed nerves even more agitated over the anticipation of the night. The last two days had passed in a blur. The Council Ball was an hour away. The door behind her opened, and she glanced at the sky one last time, studying the bright stars. It could be her last night of freedom. If she was sent to the Yards, would she see the stars again?

"Are you ready?" Jacqueline called.

Lana tore her gaze from the sky. Her parents were at the door, assessing her. She had needed a moment to clear her head, so Grant had accompanied her outside. As much as it scared her, she was ready for the night to be over, no matter the outcome.

"Yes," she answered.

Grayson's eyes met hers. "You'll be back in no time."

Lana nodded. She didn't know what to say. What could she say? There was a possibility the Council would deem her a threat and send her to the Yards. This could be the last time she would see her parents. Even if everything worked out, she still had the demons to worry about. She was a ticking time bomb, and her explosion was imminent.

Before she could stop it, a tear fell down her cheek. She brushed it away but more followed. Jacqueline wrapped her arms around her, hugging her tight.

"You're stronger than this," she whispered, pulling away to look at her. "You're stronger than them."

Grayson put his arm around Lana's shoulders. If only Jacqueline and Grayson had been approved to accompany her, she would feel so much better.

"You know..." Grayson began and then stopped, letting the thought trail off.

Lana wiped her face, pushing the tears away. She looked up at him, waiting for him to continue his thought. He looked at her, his eyes heavy.

"If something happens," he whispered. "If you don't feel right, freeze time, come back to us."

Lana's heart raced. Had she really heard him say that? Was he suggesting she run from the Council? Could she do it? Where would she go? How long would she be able to run before reapers were sent after her? Was she willing to run for the rest of her life? Were they willing to run with her?

Jacqueline glanced at Grant, making sure he wasn't listening. "He's right. Come back. We'll run together. We won't leave you."

Lana thought about what they were saying. They were willing to give up the rest of their lives for her. To go on the run, hide from the Council, the reapers. While it was a nice sentiment, she didn't think she could do that to them. She wouldn't let them give up their lives.

"It won't come to that."

"Everything will be fine," Grayson agreed. "Just stay with Terris."

Lana nodded. She hugged them one last time, wishing the

moment would last forever, that she could stay in their safe embrace. But like all good things, the moment ended too soon. She wiped the remaining tears off her face and made her way to the bathroom. She knew she would only have a few moments to put herself back together, to calm herself.

When she was alone, she turned on the faucet, letting the cool water run down the drain. She cupped her hands underneath the stream, watching it pool. The water began spilling over the top of her fingers but instead of reaching the sink, it slowly froze, the line of ice climbing. She stepped back and the ice melted, dissolving into water again.

Lana turned off the faucet and placed her hands on the counter, leaning over it. Had she really seen the water freeze? Had it been her nerves playing tricks on her? An omen, warning her how the night would go? Either way, it hadn't been a good sign.

She ran a hand through her hair, her fingers gliding through the slick ponytail before adjusting the crown on her head. She hadn't wanted to wear it. She wanted to blend in, but Ramos insisted.

Her heart hammered in her chest as she left the bathroom. Even though her feet were moving it didn't feel as if she were controlling them.

"There you are," Deliah said. "Where have you been? Dad's leaving. Oh no, your face is so red. Are you okay?"

Lana's hands flew to her cheeks. She pressed her palms over her eyes, hoping to clear them. Was this another sign the night wouldn't end well? She couldn't even look the part of an average princess.

"I'm fine."

Deliah rolled her eyes. "I know you're fine. You just don't look like you're going to a ball, to meet the Council."

Lana bit her cheek, trying to hold back tears. Why didn't her cousin understand that her invitation to the Council Ball wasn't something to be excited about? She didn't want to meet the Council. This wasn't a fun event.

"I don't care how I look," Lana said. "I just want it to be over."

Deliah took her hand. "Follow me."

Lana reluctantly followed her cousin down the hall, to the living room. Deliah made her way to her things, withdrawing a small velvet bag. She carefully untied it and reached inside, pulling out a tube of tinted moisturizer and lip gloss.

"Here," Deliah said, tossing the lip gloss to Lana. "This will only take a moment. They can wait."

Deliah dipped her fingers into the moisturizer. Lana closed her eyes as her cousin spread the mixture on her face. When she was done, she took the lip gloss and opened it, carefully running it along Lana's lips. She capped the lip gloss and stepped back, admiring her work.

"You look great."

Lana smiled. "Thank you."

"We'll miss you," Deliah said, putting the moisturizer and lip gloss away. "I can't believe I'm stuck with Dominic all night. What am I going to do?"

"You have my parents to keep you company."

Deliah's hands fell to her side. As if on instinct, Lana hugged her. She wasn't sure why she was so emotional. Everything would be fine. She would be back by the end of the night. There was no reason to begin goodbyes now.

"Are you sure you're okay?" Deliah asked, pulling away from the hug. "Why are you acting strange?"

"No reason," Lana said, wiping her eyes again. "I'm fine."

Deliah watched her in concern. Lana ran her hands down her dress, looking away from her cousin's prying eyes. Her charm bracelet snagged the fabric. She let out the breath she had been holding as she freed it from her dress.

"Are you ready?" Terris asked, joining them from the hall.

Lana turned around and found her friend near the door, his arms crossed over his chest. He was dressed in black, his pants and robe looked new. They were pressed, not a wrinkle to be found. Around his neck was a pearl necklace, the same necklace that had been given to him by her grandfather. He hadn't worn it since the night they found the Crystal in the fireplace, and in an odd way it comforted her. It almost felt as if she were her old self, just a girl from Mt. Sinclair, making her way in an unfamiliar world.

She nodded, unable to talk. Even though she hadn't really felt ready, she didn't have a choice. Terris slowly walked to her, stopping when he was before her.

"You're nervous," he said. "Don't be."

Lana nodded. Her heart raced and she took another deep breath, trying to steady her nerves. There was no use being nervous now, it wouldn't help her get through the evening.

"You look nice," he added.

Lana didn't know if it was the deep breathing or her friend's presence that began to calm her. Her head cleared and a new sense of confidence overcame her.

"You don't look so bad yourself," she said. "Thank you, for always being here for me. Even when I'm a terrible friend."

"You're not a terrible friend," he said, leading her out of the room. "Well, maybe a little."

Lana chuckled at that. A wide grin lit up his face and she knew he had only been joking. Ramos and Charlotte were waiting for them at the portal in the hall disguised as a painting. Charlotte's plum-colored gown perfectly matched her husband's cloak. They were also wearing their crowns.

"We're going to be late," Charlotte said, her eyes darting to Lana.

"Have fun," Deliah called from the living room, Dominic by her side.

"See you later," he added.

Emeric stepped out of the kitchen. He mumbled something to himself before joining them. He stopped at the portal. Without a word, he stepped into it, disappearing from view.

"After you," Ramos said, stepping aside to let them pass.

Lana took one last look behind her, expecting to see her parents. When they didn't appear, she followed Emeric, relieved that she didn't have to repeat their goodbye. She found herself in the sea of silver and pushed herself forward, through the viscous material. In the distance, she saw Emeric and followed his lead. A faint light appeared before her and she nearly ran to it, excited to leave the space in-between.

When Lana stepped out of the portal she was in a small room. Before her was a long wooden table. A white door was behind the table, a man in a gold uniform standing guard. She heard Terris behind her and turned, surprised to see a long row of mirrors behind them. Ramos and Charlotte appeared a moment later.

"You're late," the man said. "Names?"

Charlotte glared at Ramos, frustrated that they were late. Emeric made his way closer to the guard. As he gave them their names, Lana used the moment to study the room. Charlotte cleared her throat loudly, annoyed by the inconvenience at having to wait.

The guard's eyes bore into them as if scanning them, studying each person intently. Lana's mind raced, wondering what was happening. A moment later, the man nodded. He opened the door and allowed Emeric passage before gesturing everyone else through.

"What was he doing?" Lana whispered.

Terris leaned close. "Checking our intentions." When Lana frowned, he continued, "He can read our countenances. He can tell if we're here to harm the Council."

"Just by looking at us?"

He nodded, then gestured forward. A large, gilded mirror

stood in the middle of the room. A tall woman in a gold uniform stood next to it. She turned to look at them, her long robe was open at the collar, revealing a large tattoo. Long lines crisscrossed at the base of her neck.

"Rowan," Emeric said, holding his arms out. "I wasn't expecting you."

The woman chuckled softly, nodding at Emeric, then continued to run her eyes over everyone else in the room. "You know I much prefer the field."

"Don't all reapers?" Emeric said.

The hair on Lana's arm prickled. This woman was a reaper, hired by the Council of Elders to hunt those they wanted imprisoned in the Yards. She studied the woman's face, memorizing the placement of the freckles on her nose, the way her tattoo snaked up her neck. She hoped she would never see her again.

Lana listened as Emeric introduced everyone, too nervous to actually say anything. The woman's eyes darted from person to person. When Emeric got to Lana, Rowan's lips parted, and her tongue clicked.

"I know they're very eager to meet you."

Lana's stomach dropped, and she felt as if her feet were pulled out from underneath her. Was it a good sign they were eager to meet her? She opened her mouth to say something, anything, but nothing came out. Rowan gestured to Emeric.

"This way."

Rowan stepped aside to let them pass. As Lana walked by the reaper, a cold chill pressed against her. She quickly stepped into the glass, eager to leave the woman's presence. Almost immediately, Lana made her way into a large room, empty save for a large double door inlaid with pearl.

"Well," Charlotte began, gesturing to the doors. "What are we waiting for?"

Ramos cleared his throat loudly, looking at his wife. Emeric opened the door. Music greeted them, a violin playing a melancholic song.

Lana exhaled an audible gasp at the opulence. A giant chandelier, dripping with emeralds, was suspended from the cathedral ceiling and marked the middle of the ballroom. Large stained-glass windows lined the far wall. Tables of fresh meat, cheese, and fruit lined the outskirts. At the far end of the room, thirteen tall chairs stood on a raised platform, each inlaid with a different gemstone. Large green plants decorated each corner of the room. Their vines spread on the walls, converging on the ceiling. White flowers dangled from the stems.

The music changed as the full orchestra began playing. Emeric led them into the crowd of excited people and Lana scanned the room, looking for the Council. An ice sculpture caught her eye and she moved closer to inspect it. Tiny flakes of gold were set into the ice.

A tap on her shoulder broke her from her reverie. She turned to find Kiernan. His lips parted. For just a moment, his eyes lit up as they swept across her. His hand lightly touched the necklace around her neck and her breath caught in her throat.

"You're wearing it," he said, his hand falling back to his side.

Lana nodded, unable to speak. Her hands reached for the necklace, her fingers curling around the star as the music played louder. Terris saw Kiernan and said hello. As they exchanged pleasantries, Lana used the time to search the room for the Council members again.

The music stopped. The musicians stood from their seated positions, their instruments on their seats. All talking ceased as guests faced the far left, where the thirteen chairs sat.

"What's happening?" she asked, turning back to Kiernan.

He gestured toward the chairs. "The Council."

Lana raised her eyebrows, wondering what he meant. No one was approaching the chairs. The crowd parted and she was separated from Ramos. As soon as he realized what happened he quickly closed the gap, joining her. Charlotte's face twisted in anger when he left her to go to Lana.

A large man, dressed in the reapers' uniform of gold, proceeded to walk toward the chairs. He stepped onto the platform and opened a paneled door that was disguised as the wall. He stepped back, his hand resting on a large sword at his waist.

An older woman with thin gray hair stepped out of the doorway. Behind her, twelve more people filed out. They each stood in front of a chair, and as one, sat. The woman on the far-right chair, who led the group, surveyed the room. She clapped her hands once. Immediately, the musicians sat down again, and picked up their instruments.

The music resumed and the guests began dancing. Ramos smiled at Lana. She knew this was it, the beginning of the Council's test and took another deep breath. Once the night was over, and she was safe in Bridian, she would go back to her main focus—the demons.

Lana forewent the dancing in favor of studying each member of the Council. The older woman was talking to the reaper, his head bowed as he intently listened to her. Lana's eyes moved down the line, counting five women and eight men, all ranging in age. They all wore champagne-colored robes. The man to the far left leaned his head back, revealing a large patch of gray skin and she quickly looked away, not wanting to be caught staring.

"Why is his skin gray, on his neck?" she whispered to her uncle, subtly pointing to the man.

Ramos didn't even look. "He's from Linnick, another dimension. Everyone born there has that mark."

Lana nodded. She turned back to the Council, discreetly looking for any other differences, anything else that set them apart and marked them from other worlds. Her gaze settled on a woman near the middle. Their eyes met, and as much as she wanted to look away, she couldn't. It was as if something was pulling her, holding her. The woman's violet eyes sparkled, and it felt as if she was reading Lana.

"Would you like to dance?" Kiernan asked.

The question pulled Lana away from the woman, her charm bracelet catching her attention and reminding her of Jacqueline and Grayson. What were they doing right now? Were they waiting for her to return?

"Yes," Lana said, accepting Kiernan's offer to dance, grateful for the distraction. "That would be nice."

Kiernan held his hand out and she took it. A brief moment of panic overcame her, and she removed her hand from his. She was already nervous. She didn't want to accidentally drain him like she had Deliah.

"Stay close," Ramos said, his eyes scanning the room. He waved to someone and then turned back to her. "Dinner will be served shortly."

Lana nodded. Kiernan led her a few feet away. He placed his hands on her waist as the music increased, a harp joining the orchestra. She had never danced with anyone before and wasn't sure where to put her hands. She looked at the other guests. Most of the women had their arms around their partner's necks, their bodies close.

Lana slowly reached up and placed her hands on Kiernan's shoulders, gently resting them on his cloak, away from his skin. "I've never danced with anyone before. Do I just follow your lead?"

Kiernan raised his left eyebrow slightly. "Ever? Were there no balls in Mt. Sinclair?"

"We had school dances," she answered. "They weren't like this."

Memories of Mt. Sinclair High School's Homecoming and Winter Formal flashed through her mind. They were so far removed from the Council Ball. No one really danced with each other. The boys spent the time showing off, running around the gymnasium, or pranking one another. The girls usually stayed in groups, gossiping, or taking selfies.

He cleared his throat. "I talked to the Council."

Lana looked up at him, following his lead as he swayed from side to side. He leaned in closer. He was so close she was sure he could smell her breath and grew self-conscious. He smelled of oranges and cinnamon and hoped she smelled just as nice.

"They prefer I wait," he continued, spinning her. "Just another year or so until they make their final decision. But they seem open to it."

Lana swallowed; her mouth suddenly dry. "Is that what you really want?"

The music changed. A slow song overtook the room, wrapping them under its spell. Kiernan slowed but didn't stop dancing.

"What do you mean?"

Lana paused before answering. "I mean, if they grant the request, you could be sent somewhere far. Somewhere away from your family. Is that what you really want?"

She remembered his grandmother and a lump formed in her throat. She didn't want him to leave his family because of her. When would she even see him? She looked away, trying to distract herself. Ramos was watching her, his eyes following their movement. Terris shifted on his feet, his arms crossed over his chest, clearly uncomfortable by himself.

Kiernan's brow furrowed. "I want to give this a chance. Even if it doesn't go anywhere, if nothing happens between us, I want to know that I gave it my all. From the moment I met you... Life is too short to live with regret."

Lana's cheeks flushed. She looked away, unsure what to say. She liked him but felt out of her element. Even though she had crushes before, no one had actually reciprocated the feelings. It was easy to like people from afar, there was no chance for heartbreak.

"I guess we'll see what they decide," he added, his gaze dropping to the floor.

Lana looked away, surprised to see how close they were to the Council. In their dancing, they had inadvertently made their way closer to the raised platform. She gripped his shoulders tight, nervous to be near the Council members.

"Can we go back?" she whispered, hoping no one heard her over the music.

Kiernan removed his hands from her waist. Without drawing too much attention, they made their way back to Ramos, whose eyes never left her. The music stopped and the woman with the gray hair stood, her hands clasped before her.

"Thank you all for being here," she said, her eyes sweeping the room.

Suddenly, another voice called out, speaking in a different language. The woman paused, clearly expecting the interruption. When the other voice had finished talking, the woman continued.

"Make your way through those doors." She pointed to a set of double doors with thin lines of what looked like gold etched around large diamonds. "We're eager to meet you all," she added, her eyes resting on Lana.

Lana's blood ran cold as the same voice began speaking. She realized it was a translator, relaying what the woman had said in another language of those in the room.

"Lana," Ramos said, stepping up to her. "Are you ready?"

"As ready as I'll ever be," she answered, her voice cracking.

She pressed her lips together tightly. Even though she wasn't sure she was ready, there was nothing she could do. Now that they were no longer dancing, she felt awkward standing so close to Kiernan. He shuffled on his feet, the same awkwardness overtaking him.

They followed the crowd through the double doors and into a large banquet room. The room had two tables, a small one to their right and a larger one before them. The room was decorated in the same fashion as the large ballroom. Her eyes swept from the emerald encrusted chandelier to the stained-glass windows.

Lana was relieved there wasn't assigned seating. She had been worried she was going to be separated from Ramos and Terris. Kiernan joined his father, who was talking to Damarius near the doors.

"These seats will do," Charlotte said. "Ramos, sit next to me, on my right. Lana will go on your right."

Charlotte pointed to three chairs, completely ignoring Terris. Lana sat, pulling the chair to her right out for her friend.

"Sit next to me."

When everyone was seated, she admired the setting before her. A large centerpiece of orange, blue, and violet flowers, unlike any she had ever seen, stood before them. Thin gold lines were painted down the veins of the bright green leaves. Each place setting had champagne-colored napkins atop gold plates. Polished gold utensils lay to the right of the plate, and frosted glasses stood on the left.

Lana placed her hands in her lap and watched those around her, waiting to follow their lead. Emeric had explained what a dinner with the Council would entail but she still felt caught off guard, scared to make a mistake.

"Remember what we went over," Emeric said, leaning over her right shoulder.

Lana nodded and he stepped backward, making his way to a chair next to an older man in a black suit, a white kerchief in his breast pocket. As those around her settled into conversation, she closed her eyes and steadied her breathing. She could do this. Once dinner was over, there would be time for the

Council to meet their guests. That's what she had to worry about, not the actual dinner.

She opened her eyes and took the napkin off her plate and unwrapped it, placing it on her lap. Terris drummed his fingers on the table, her nervous energy overtaking him. The Council entered, taking their seats at the smaller table, followed by a staff of five. They dispersed, going to different sections of the room, filling water glasses.

Lana reached for her glass of water, bringing it to her lips. Ramos tapped her on the shoulder, subtly clearing his throat. She turned to him, and he shook his head, looking at the glass in her hands. Emeric's training came back to her, and she remembered it was impolite to eat or drink first. That honor was reserved for the Council.

She carefully, but swiftly, placed the glass back on the table. Her eyes swept the room, hoping no one had seen her indiscretion. The energy in the room shifted as the servers left. All talking stopped as the Council members' eyes swept the room, studying their guests.

"I was quite enjoying the conversation," a younger Council member said, leaning back in his chair, his hands steepled in front of him. "No need to stop on our account."

A few quiet chuckles erupted as the servers reappeared. They carried covered trays and set them on the table. Lana's eyes widened at the amount of food they brought out, occupying the large table. Then the servers brought glass carafes, filled with amber liquid. Her frosted glass was filled, and she wondered what the liquid was, but was too nervous to ask.

The woman with the gray hair stood. The other Council members looked out at their guests. Lana immediately bowed her head, trying to avoid eye contact.

"As the longest serving member of the Council, I thank you for joining us this evening," she said, her voice high, forcing herself to sound grateful. "I've served on the Council for fifty-seven years. When my father stepped down, the position passed to me, the eldest Elingston. It's been an honor to serve you. To protect those that cannot protect themselves." She paused, allowing the interpreter to speak. "In my fifty-seven years, I have helped put away some of the most dangerous criminals. I know I speak for all when I say we do it for you. Thank you for joining us, for celebrating our accomplishments."

Lana listened to the interpreter. Even though she couldn't understand the language, she knew it was the message she had already heard. She had a hard time digesting it, the lie. They weren't protecting those that couldn't protect themselves. They let Alderic escape. When they found out that he was no longer in the Yards, that someone else was in his cell, they kept it quiet. She couldn't trust them, despite their show of faith.

A round of applause echoed throughout the room when the translator had finished. The anger inside Lana raged. How could everyone be so blind to it? One look around the room and she knew the Council was out for themselves. The opulence, the decadence. Even though she had only seen two rooms, she guessed the rest of the Council's building was just as grand. While Alderic was loose, they were having balls.

"Lana?" Ramos whispered, his face pale. "What's wrong?"

Lana couldn't answer. As the applause died down, she twisted the ring around her finger, counting how many times it spun. She kept her gaze in front of her, trying to remain calm. She had the wherewithal to know that it was the demons. Her emotions were heightened, and she was on edge, but it wasn't her. It was them. They were putting thoughts in her head.

"Not only is this a celebration of our good work throughout the years," the woman continued. "This is a celebration of you."

"All right, Lorelle," the younger man said, teasing the older woman. "Let's get on with it. We're all hungry, right?"

There was more applause as Lorelle reached for her frosted

glass with the amber-colored drink. She raised it high in the air, smiling widely.

"To you," she said. "For your unwavering support of our cause."

All around her, people picked up their cups. As the Council members cheered, clinking their glasses together, the guests followed suit. Next to her, Ramos picked up his glass.

"This isn't right," she said, her voice louder than necessary. "He's still out there. The demons are inside me. The Council isn't doing anything to help except makes speeches."

Ramos narrowed his eyes at her. "Pick up your glass."

She shook her head, angry that he would even suggest that. She didn't understand. Why was he on their side, playing along with the lie? They weren't doing anything. From what she could tell, all they did was sit in their luxurious chairs while reapers hunted down those they deemed unworthy.

"No," she said, her voice laced with venom. "I'm not going to celebrate them. Not until they prove there's something to celebrate."

Ramos set his glass down before leaning close to her. "Not now. This isn't the place. Play their game and we leave. Even if you don't like it, play along."

Lana swallowed. The anger inside her was taking its roots, spreading where it could. She picked up her glass and held it high in the air. But instead of celebrating the Council, she vowed to take them down. She was going to find out exactly how Alderic escaped, and why they weren't doing anything to find him.

**10**

———

# THE DAGGER

Lana watched a thin line of frost spread across the table, toward her plate. She picked up her napkin and threw it on top, trying to conceal it. She reached for her glass, using the opportunity to look around the table, hoping that no one had seen. As she sipped the cool water, her eyes darted left to right. No one's eyes met hers.

"Everything okay?" Terris leaned close, keeping his attention on his meal in an effort to camouflage their discussion.

Lana set her glass down, thankful that the frost hadn't spread. Even though she was beginning to slip, and wasn't acting like herself, she didn't want to concern him. The last thing she needed was for everyone to worry. In a way, that would make it worse. She didn't have the energy to deal with other people at the moment.

"Everything's fine. Can you pass the bread?"

Terris slid the basket to her. Her hand brushed against the wicker, and she noticed tiny pearls set inside the weave. Even though she wasn't hungry, she had another use for it. She set the warm slice of bread on the napkin, hoping the warmth would melt the frost underneath. Terris watched but didn't say anything. Charlotte's voice caught her attention.

"Look how attentive they are."

Confused, Lana turned to look at her aunt, wondering who she was talking about. The Council? The rest of the guests? Charlotte was pointing to the servers, who were stationed throughout the room. Even though it was expected from her aunt, Lana's stomach sank, hoping that Terris hadn't heard. She stole a glance at her friend. His head was down, focused on his plate.

Before she could say anything, apologize for her aunt, the room fell silent. Lorelle was standing, her long fingers holding a diamond encrusted glass. Her eyes darted across the room, stopping on a man near the front.

"Magnum Lantz," she said, her voice high. "You made our job quite easy. I knew that you would be too proud to pass up the opportunity to attend."

The man flinched. He pushed his chair back, as if he were going to flee. Reapers appeared at the doors. When the man realized there was no way out, he fell to his knees and clasped his hands in front of him, his long-braided hair touching the floor behind him.

"This is all a misunderstanding," he pled. "Whatever it is you think I did—"

Lorelle set the glass on the table in front of her. "Enough. I do hope you enjoyed the meal."

The reapers marched in. When the man didn't move, two reapers approached him and stood on either side of him, lifting him in the air. The room was so tense the hair on Lana's arm stood at end. What was happening? Was she dreaming? The man shouted, pleading to be spared as he was taken out of the room.

No one moved. The silence was deafening. Lorelle looked out at her guests once more. A smile spread across her face.

"It's been a pleasure dining with you."

She turned, exiting through the door behind the table. The rest of the Council stood. They followed her.

Lana's head spun. What had just happened? Was that it? Was it over? Could they leave? The room was so quiet she could hear the servers moving the carts in the hall.

"What just happened?" Lana turned to her uncle, whispering. "Who was that man? Why did they take him?"

Terris leaned over her plate, so close she felt his breath on her neck. He had been just as confused and scared as she was. Ramos exhaled the pent-up breath he had been holding before answering.

"I've only met him a handful of times in passing. He's from Maldenium. He's their Magnum."

"Magnum?" Lana's voice cracked. "What's that?"

"An elected official," Ramos answered, looking around the room nervously. "It's his land's highest position. I don't know what he did, but it must have been significant."

Lana tried to calm her racing thoughts. Her heartbeat echoed in her ears, the pressure making her dizzy.

"Are they taking him to the Yards?" Terris asked.

Ramos set his napkin on his plate. "I don't know."

Quiet conversation resumed. Everyone had been just as confused. The happy, cheerful atmosphere obliterated in a matter of moments. Lana's eyes darted to the doors, expecting the Council to rejoin them.

"Can we go? Is it over?"

Ramos shook his head. "No. The Council has retired to their private chambers. They'll call on guests in the order they wish to speak to them."

Lana felt the air leave her again. She couldn't imagine speaking to the Council after that public display. She couldn't imagine what they were like in private.

Seeing the change on her face, Ramos said, "We'll be on our way before you know it."

In the hall, the music resumed. Everyone slowly made their way out of the dining room, following the sound. Lana slid her chair back, more than ready to finish the night, to put the show of support for the Council behind her. She followed Ramos, wondering what the point of this was. To show everyone how important they were? To remind everyone how powerful they are?

A reaper stepped in through the door the Council members had exited from. He scanned the room as he walked toward Lana and Ramos. Lana stepped back, allowing him space to pass. Instead of walking past her, he came to an abrupt stop.

"Princess Lana of Bridian?"

Lana looked at her uncle. When he nodded, she said, "Yes?"

The reaper relaxed his stance. "The Council would like to meet with you now."

Lana's breath caught in her throat. Even though she knew it would happen, that she would meet them before they left, she thought she would have more time to prepare. Why were they calling on her first?

"I've been in contact with the Council," Ramos said, stepping forward. "They've agreed to let me accompany her."

"King Ramos," the man said, looking him over. "Come with me."

Ramos followed the man, gesturing to Lana to do the same. She hadn't even had time to say anything to Terris or Kiernan, both of whom were watching the exchange silently. Terris offered her a strained smile of encouragement.

"I'll see you soon."

Lana couldn't bring herself to say anything. She didn't want to say goodbye, so she didn't.

"Save me another dance?" Kiernan asked.

She nodded, words failing her. Lana quickly turned away.

Her feet were weak, silently protesting each step, warning her to retreat. Against her better judgment, she caught up to the reaper, skirting around pockets of confused people, trying to piece together what had happened.

The reaper led them up the raised platform. He walked past the table toward the door at the back. She glanced where the Council sat, their plates were still full, piled with food. Why hadn't they eaten anything? What was the point of dinner if they weren't going to eat?

They stepped through the doorway into a long hallway. Crystal sconces lined the wall, a soft glow leading the way. When the hall split, the reaper led them to the right, deeper into the building. She memorized their path, counting the steps in her head, so she could find her way back to her friends.

A moment later, the reaper stopped at a dark wood door lined in iridescent pearl. He knocked once before opening it, stepping aside to let them pass. Ramos turned to look at Lana, taking her hand and squeezing it tight. She stepped inside the brightly lit room.

"Ah," a male voice said. "Our first visitors."

"How are you enjoying the night?" another asked.

Ramos answered and Lana let her eyes adjust to the bright room. Lorelle sat on a tall hardback chair, her posture perfect, back straight, and arms crossed on her lap. Next to her, a younger man leaned against the back of the chair. He watched Lana, expressionless. The rest of the Council members were spread about the room, some on a large couch, while others rested on chairs. One was even standing at the window with his back to her.

"Tell us what happened when you broke the Crystal," the man leaning against Lorelle's chair asked.

"Elex," Lorelle said. "Let's not overwhelm her."

He pushed off the chair, standing tall. All eyes were on Lana, and she didn't know what was expected. Should she do something? Say something? Answer his question? Shouldn't they already know the answer anyway?

Ramos stepped forward. "Thank you for extending the invitation. It's an honor."

Elex narrowed his eyes, as if finally noticing Ramos. "And you are?"

"Don't be rude," the woman with the violet eyes said. "This must be King Ramos Morgan, Lana's uncle, Alderic's brother. My name's Elora."

"It's a pleasure to meet you," Ramos said.

Elex turned back to Lana. "Well, how did you enjoy dinner?"

Lana's eyes swept the room, gauging how to answer. "It was an experience."

Elex chuckled. "We should have offered dessert, right?" This wasn't the response she had been expecting and didn't know how to answer. Elex spoke to the man near the window, who had his back to them. "Gideon, I told you we should have offered dessert."

Gideon slowly turned around, the gray circle on his neck visible. His eyes focused on Lana. He ignored Elex, instead taking a step forward.

"Let's not waste time, shall we?" he asked, turning from Lana. "There's a reason we wanted to meet the girl. Let's get on with it."

A woman with tightly curled blonde hair stood, her eyes darting to the rest of her companions. "There's time. Look at her, she's scared."

"Sit down, Genevieve," Gideon said. "We don't have time. We still need to take the Magnum to the Yards. I'd like to get home at some point tonight."

Genevieve narrowed her eyes at Gideon but sat, crossing her arms over her chest tightly. Lana's head spun. She hadn't been expecting the Council to fight. She had been expecting a united front. Maybe she could use it to her advantage. She had questions that she wanted answers to.

"What did he do?" she asked, her voice small.

The Council members were quiet, caught off guard. Lana clenched her fingers into tight balls, trying to steady her nerves. Now that she had asked the question, she wondered if it had been a mistake. Maybe she could pull it back as she had done before.

Elex chuckled again. "I like her. She's confident."

Lana wouldn't call it confidence. She was the least confident person she knew. It was more that she didn't know better. She had been shocked at her brazenness. She didn't know where it came from but hoped it didn't leave her.

"Confident?" Gideon said, addressing Elex. "Or ignorant?"

"It's not your concern," Lorelle's harsh voice interrupted, looking at Lana.

"I apologize for my niece," Ramos said. "I'm afraid I haven't taught her the proper protocol. She had been in the dark for years of her birthright. She just recently learned the truth."

Lana stared at him. He kept his gaze straight and wouldn't acknowledge her. Why was he doing this? It had only been a question.

"We know all about her past," an older man with salt and pepper hair said. "I think I speak for all when I say that I'm more interested in the present. Johan's account is very concerning." All eyes convened at Lana again. She paused, waiting to see if Ramos would answer. He opened his mouth, but the man held up his hand, silencing him. "I'd like to hear Lana's account."

Ramos looked at Lana, encouraging her to answer. Her mind went blank. She couldn't think of anything to say. What could she say? That the demons happened to overpower her at that moment? Explain that she was slowly losing herself to them.

"I wasn't feeling well that day."

Elex scoffed. "Is that all?"

"Come on, Judah, you don't believe that do you?" Gideon said to the older man before turning to the rest of the Council members. "Does anyone?"

Lorelle turned her sharp gaze on Lana. "Tell us more."

Lana swallowed, turning over possible answers in her head. Everyone's eyes were trained on her, making her uncomfortable. When she finally settled on one, she said, "I don't remember much. Maybe I had the flu."

As soon as the words were out of her mouth, she realized they may not know what a flu was. She shifted on her feet, the tension in the room palpable.

"It was just bad timing," Ramos added quickly, before he could be silenced again.

Ramos hadn't been lying. It had been bad timing. She had just learned that the Council had denied their request to see Amos. She had been caught off guard, she didn't understand the reason for their decision. She looked up, biting her tongue to keep from asking for an explanation as it would only make things worse.

"The demons pose no threat. You have control over them?" Lorelle asked, her sharp gaze on Lana.

Lana's mouth ran dry. How was she supposed to answer? Her brain went blank, forgetting everything Emeric had coached her on. Her hands trembled and she ran them down her cloak.

"We're only here to help," Lorelle added.

Something about her tone let Lana know it had been a lie. They weren't here to help. They were looking after themselves. They proved that when they made the decision to keep Alderic's escape private. They didn't want the negative press.

"I've always been in control," Lana answered, resting her

hands on her hips, her thoughts shifting. "Isn't that even more reason to help me?"

Gideon threw his hands up. "What is this? We all heard Johan's account."

"That's why we asked to meet you," Lorelle said, ignoring Gideon's outburst. "We want to help."

Lana knew it was too good to be true. Had they changed their mind? Were they going to allow her to speak to Amos? Had they already spoken to him?

"Can I speak to him?" she asked, her voice a whisper. "To Amos?"

Lorelle's eyebrows furrowed. "You don't know what you're asking."

"Out of the question," Gideon said.

Elex stepped forward. "You're so young, so naïve. Let us do our jobs. Let us figure this out."

Lana bit her tongue. Elex hadn't looked that much older than her. She wanted to say something. She wanted to ask them what they were doing to find Alderic. She wanted to ask what they were doing to help her with the demons. The fire inside her raged, but instead of acting on it she remained silent.

"What are you doing?" Ramos asked, surprising Lana at his frankness. "What are you doing to help find my brother?"

"Now, now." Gideon waved him away. "We don't answer to you."

"Forgive me," Ramos said. "I only ask as I fear for our safety. Lana's safety."

"I didn't think Alderic was a threat to your safety," Genevieve said. "Now that the Crystal is destroyed. What more can he do?"

Lana clenched her fists. Did they think that was the end of her problems? That everything was fine now that the Crystal had been destroyed? It seemed as if they weren't going to help, and she closed her eyes, wishing she could be alone, wishing she could go home.

The room was silent for longer than she had been expecting and she opened her eyes. Everyone was still, frozen in time. She turned to her uncle, shaking her head in disbelief when she saw he was frozen as well. What had happened? Had she stopped time again? She hadn't meant to.

She stepped closer to Ramos, touching his arm. When he didn't move, she spun around, studying the Council members, making sure they were all frozen. She was standing in a room with what looked like wax statues. Only these statues were real, and she didn't know when they would awake.

A wicked idea overtook her, one that she couldn't shake. Was the entrance to the Yards close? While they couldn't stop her, maybe she could look for a key. Her heart hammered in her chest as she stepped closer to Lorelle, waving her hand before her face to be sure they were really frozen.

Her eyes darted across the room, looking for anything of importance. Even though the room was extravagant by Lana's standards, she noticed there was no other furniture besides the chairs and a desk. There were no tables, armoires, or even shelves. Crystal sconces lined the walls, lighting the room. Plush blue curtains framed the polished window, and the walls were lined in white textured wallpaper. Although the room was beautiful, it was only used for meetings, it couldn't be the Council's office.

A surge of adrenaline raced through her, the excitement invigorating her. She knew the Council members could unfreeze at any moment. Keeping her eyes peeled for any movement, she made her way to the desk, walking between Lorelle and Elex. The first thing that drew her attention was the lamp. Citrine and sapphire jewels hung from the delicate lampshade, casting sparkles onto the polished wood. Besides the lamp, the surface was clear.

Lana's hands shook as she reached for the top drawer. She pulled it open to find a stack of thick blank parchment paper. She reached inside, running her thumb along the pages. They were all blank. She closed the drawer and moved to the next. She sighed, finding nothing of importance, nothing that would help her.

The room was quiet as she turned around, facing the Council members' backs. How much longer would they be frozen? What if they didn't unfreeze? She pushed the thoughts out of her mind. She scanned the room, searching for anything she may have missed.

She stepped forward, moving in between Lorelle and Elex again. She was standing before Ramos. She placed her hand on his, willing with all her might that he would wake up, leaving the rest frozen. When he didn't move, she thought of Kiernan and Terris. Were they frozen as well? Was it just those in this room or did it extend to everyone else?

Lana couldn't shake the feeling that someone was watching her. A shiver ran down her spine as her eyes darted across the room again. The hair on her arms prickled when she realized that everyone was still frozen, the feeling overtaking her. She ran to the door and pulled it open. She looked down the hall, but no one was there. She was alone.

A low ringing echoed in her ears and her stomach dropped. She walked back into the room, closing the door behind her. As the ringing grew louder, she leaned against the wall, barely able to stand. A man's voice sent another chill down her spine.

"Look for the folder."

Lana spun around but didn't see anyone. Had she really heard it? Was someone else in the room with her? Or had she only imagined it? She stumbled forward, almost tripping over her feet when she saw the folder on Judah's lap.

All at once the ringing stopped. The folder beckoned her. She stepped forward. Judah's long fingers sat atop the matte black file. There was nothing written on the cover, but she had to know what was inside. The curiosity was overwhelming, and she reached down, grasping the file in her hands. She slowly pulled it toward her. She had expected him to protest, to pull the file back, but she met no opposition.

She turned the file in her hands, realizing she had been looking at the back. Written in small cursive handwriting was *Carlecia Morgan/Lana Laughlin*. Why was her name written on it?

With trembling hands, she opened the cover. An envelope fell to the floor, but she was too preoccupied to bother with it. The first thing she saw was a detailed report from Johan, the Council messenger, describing what he had seen when he delivered the letter. She skimmed through it, almost dropping the entire file when she got to the end.

*I firmly believe that something else had overtaken her, something dark.*

Before she lost her nerve, she rifled through the rest of the pages. She saw a letter from Ramos, explaining the events from the night of his birthday and asking the Council for help. Behind the letter, she found a copy of their response.

*While we understand the severity of the situation, it is imperative we do not create mass panic. No one has escaped the Yards before and our best reapers are looking for him. He won't get far.*

Her breathing became heavy as she reread their response. To her, it didn't make sense. Against her better judgment, she continued to look through the file, finding her uncle's letter detailing the night the Crystal broke, pleading for any kind of help they could send.

"Aren't you going to look at the envelope?"

Lana jumped at the voice. The file flew from her hands, the pages spilling at her feet. Her arms flew to her chest when she saw the young man before her. She hadn't heard him enter; he wasn't one of the Council members. Relief washed over her when she realized the Council members were all frozen, still suspended in time.

"Who are you?"

The man chuckled, the ends of his mouth pulling up in a crooked smile. "My name's not important. An envelope fell from the file when you opened it. Are you going to read it?"

Lana's head dipped as she looked at the letter lying near her feet. She looked up to find the man watching her, his eyes lit. He stood taller, stretching his shoulders as if he had been sitting too long. The hair on her arms prickled as she realized she had seen him before; she just couldn't place where.

"Who are you?" she repeated. "Do you work for the Council?"

"No," he answered simply. "You can call me whatever you like."

Lana's head was spinning. Who was he? Where had he come from? Why wouldn't he tell her his name?

"I didn't hear the door open."

The man's head tilted to the left. "Are you sure about that? You were there, the night I was called."

Lana placed her hands on her temples, trying to calm the anger inside her. The man and his riddles weren't helping the situation. She wasn't in the mood for games. She wanted answers. She bent down and picked up the envelope. It seemed as if he wanted it. Maybe he would leave her alone if she gave it to him. She held it out.

"Here. Will you leave me alone now?"

"I don't want that," he answered. "I have no use for paper."

Lana pulled her arm back when a name on the envelope caught her attention. *Shandra VanDriesen.* Why was there an envelope in her file with Shandra's name on it? She turned it over and saw that the letter was carefully opened. A thin slit at the top revealed a folded letter. She slid it out of the envelope. *My dearest Shandra* was written on top. She scanned the letter and saw it was signed by Amos.

*The rumors about the dagger are spreading. Harken's great grandfather was a Revatto. He remembers stories of a treasure, hidden in the caves. When Alderic frees me, we'll find it. We can use it to release them. We don't need the girl any longer. In fact, when we find the dagger, we may be able to take the magic out of her.*

Lana turned the paper over, looking for the rest but it was blank. That was it? What dagger was he talking about? How could they take the magic out of her? How did the Council get their hands on the letter? Her hands shook as the man stepped forward, his arms limp at his waist.

"Was it important?"

Lana looked up at him. "Who are you? How did you know about this?"

The man ran his tongue across his teeth, accentuating the act, as if he wasn't used to them. His dark brown eyes lit up.

"I've been with you the past few weeks. I know what you're looking for, the answers that you seek. I only wagered a guess that it was important."

Lana's blood ran cold. How could he have been with her the last few weeks? How did he know what she was looking for? She stepped back, her eyes darting to Ramos, still frozen. She held her arm out, willing that time would restart. The man took another step closer, only this time when he walked, a thin layer of frost shot out from each foot, gliding across the floor toward her. Like a flash, an image appeared before her. She had seen the man before. When the demons overpowered her. It had been more than a dream. He was one of them.

"I don't understand," she said, her voice barely a whisper. "I've seen the demons before. They didn't look like you. They didn't look like people."

"We appear how we want to appear," he answered. "We aren't limited to one form."

The frost inched its way closer, slowly crawling along the floor. She stepped back again, her mind processing it all. It didn't make sense. How could it?

"But I'm not really here," he said, disappearing into thin air.

Lana's head flew in every direction, looking for him. The frost melted, the only evidence of his presence. The room was quiet. Suddenly, he reappeared next to her. He was so close, their shoulders touched.

"I'm in here," he said, pointing to her head.

Lana jumped. The letter dropped to the floor and the man picked it up. His eyes darted across it.

"How?" she asked. "How am I seeing you? What do you want?"

"We want the same thing. We want our lives back." The man cleared his throat. "I know you want to give your friend his magic back. You want to be *normal*."

As much as she wanted to move, to run and never look back, she was rooted. His mere presence held her in his orbit. He offered her the letter.

"He's right," he continued. "About the dagger. There's enough sacrificial magic shrouding it to release us."

She took the letter back, rereading it, trying to make sense of it. When she reached the end, she was just as confused. The man bent, so his face was close to hers. Lana wanted to step away. To her relief, he straightened so they were no longer face-to-face.

"We're very much alike," he said, his lips pulled to one side. "We were both torn from our lives, our homes, for someone else."

"When Alderic called you here?"

The man scoffed. "That wasn't the first time."

"King Mathias?" she said. "He called you first. Is it true? That wasn't just speculation?"

Lana learned of King Mathias in Alderic's journal. There were rumors that he called on something dark, something evil, after the death of his son. She looked up at the man, meeting his hard gaze.

"We're not that bad," he said. "We didn't invade this world; we were brought here. When he tired of us, he killed himself. It did send us home though, until it happened a second time."

Lana's mind turned, trying to make sense of it. Frost pooled at their feet. Was he talking about King Mathias? When he died, Medora prospered once more. He had killed himself?

"How were you sent back?"

"His death severed our connection," he answered. "He had called us, there was no additional tether. No anchor to hold us."

Lana was their tether. Alderic believed King Mathias had called them but hadn't tethered them correctly. There had been nothing to keep them in line, King Mathias couldn't control them. He needed an innocent.

If what he was saying was true, even though King Mathias had been unable to control them, he had been able to send them back, with his death. Would that mean they could be sent back now, if Alderic died? He had called them.

"If Alderic dies, does that mean you'll be sent back?" she asked, holding her breath to hear his answer.

The man sighed. "No. You are our tether. His death would mean nothing to us."

That wasn't the answer she had wanted. She realized she had been clenching her fist and relaxed her fingers.

"King Mathias wanted to send you back so badly he killed himself?"

His eyes swept through the room, looking at the Council

members. "He was angry he couldn't control us, sate our appetite."

Lana's stomach fell. "Your appetite?"

He smiled. "People. Their anger, confusion, pain. It feeds us." Lana swallowed, stepping back, away from him, but he continued. "Can you guess the one emotion that's the sweetest, the one we crave above all others?"

Lana shook her head. She couldn't even answer, too afraid to hear his response.

"Fear," he continued. "But to get that, to pull that out, usually killed the person. King Mathias was angry. He blamed us, even though he was the one that called us. His gamble worked. He figured out the one way he could send us home. We were ready for it anyway. We were running out of people."

Lana's eyes grew wide. Why was he telling her this? She took another step backward, her eyes searching the room for something to use in case he attacked her.

"If I die, will that send you back?" Her voice trembled as she spoke.

Lana wasn't sure she was ready to hear his answer. While she wanted to be free from them, was she really ready to die?

"Not quite." He turned from her. "If you die, and we're still trapped here, inside of you, we die. Right now, we're a part of you. But if we had the dagger, you could release us. The ceremony could be finished, the sacrifice made. Then you would have the power to send us home."

Sacrifice? Lana couldn't even speak the word. Did he really think that she would kill someone to release them?

As if he read her mind, he clarified, "No actual sacrifice has to be made. The dagger is coated in enough sacrificial blood. The magic stayed with it. King Mathias's ultimate sacrifice, as well as the original, the one that brought us here. That's why we need it. That's why you need to be the one to find it."

Lana bit her lips, her eyes roaming, still searching for

something to use if he attacked. Could she even outrun him? Her best bet was to keep him talking, to learn everything she could.

"King Mathias's dagger?"

"Yes," he said, his voice low. "When we were pulled the second time, the ceremony was interrupted. There was no sacrifice made. We were pulled into that Crystal, too far in this world to be sent back, but without the necessary steps to be free. The dagger possesses enough sacrificial magic to truly release us."

Lana's gaze fell to the letter at her feet. Amos's words haunting her. *We can use it to release them. We don't need the girl any longer.*

"Alderic didn't need me after all?" Lana asked. "If he had the dagger, he could have released you from the Crystal without me?"

He nodded. "We would still have been tethered to you."

Lana processed this information in her mind, trying to unpack it. The man before her didn't look like a demon, at least not in the sense she had been expecting. Was he actually trying to help? Why?

"Why me?" Lana asked. "Why do I have to find it? Why are you helping me?"

He pinched the bridge of his nose, annoyed with her questions. "Just as we're tied to you, you're tied to us. We want our freedom. The dagger should be able to release us, but we don't want just anyone to have that honor. They'll have the power to control us, make us do what they want." His eyes trained on hers again. "You want to send us home. You see, we want the same thing."

Lana shivered. If what he was saying was true, she could send them back. Then another thought sprang to mind.

"Will I have to die? If we find the dagger and free you, won't I have to die to send you home?"

"No," his voice hissed, echoing in the large room. "You won't have to die. There are other ways."

Lana didn't know if she believed him. It sounded too good to be true. He was handing her the information she needed. Maybe they could find the dagger. He could tell her how to finish the ceremony and send them home.

"When I broke the Crystal," Lana asked, her voice cracking. "Why couldn't I send you home? Why did you go into me?"

His sharp eyes bore into her again. "You weren't strong enough. You didn't know what you were doing. As our tether, you were the first place that called to us. Rather unfortunate, you're the last place I want to be."

"King Mathias called you hundreds of years ago," Lana said, her eyes narrowed, trying to think clearly. "How are you even alive? How were you called back?"

He shrugged. "We don't age as you do."

The frost continued to spread. She looked away from him, her gaze setting on Ramos. So many questions still raced through her. The room grew cold.

"The quickest way to find the dagger is to let us in," he said. "Stop fighting us."

There it was. She knew that he wanted something, something she wasn't willing to give. Sweat pooled on her forehead.

"No," she said, looking around the room again, willing everyone to unfreeze. "You did this. What did you do to them?"

He put his hands behind his back. "I only wished to speak to you. To help."

The air around him shimmered, almost as if he was a projection about to disappear. He froze, his face contorted, as if in pain. A moment later, he looked up again, then walked right into her.

It happened so fast she was caught off guard. Her hands flew up in an attempt to shield herself. Her screams echoed; her throat raw. She fell backward, her body shaking. Even though she had lost herself to the darkness before, this felt different.

"There we go," the demon's voice slithered in her mind. "Don't fight it."

Another deep guttural scream escaped her lips. Her muscles tensed and she closed her eyes, trying to shut out the pain. She fell backward and her head hit the cold floor. Silence replaced her screams. When the pain finally subsided, she came to, but something was off. She was no longer in control of her own body. Her thoughts were clouded, no longer only hers. It was as if she were drawing from the darkness. She was now standing but didn't remember actually getting up.

"Lana," Ramos said.

His brow was furrowed, trying to piece together what happened.

"How did you get over there?" Gideon asked.

Judah gasped. "The folder. How did you get that?"

Lana wanted to warn them, tell them to run but the words wouldn't come. She raised her arms, palms facing the ceiling.

"Don't do this Lana," Ramos warned.

"Stop her!" Lorelle said.

Before anyone could do anything, and against her better judgment, Lana vanished into a thick black mist.

**11**

---

## THE DARKNESS WITHIN

Lana knew it was wrong, that she shouldn't leave the Council. She was handing them the proof they needed to send her to the Yards. But something compelled her, and she couldn't stop. She was propelled, as if in a speeding car she couldn't escape, a dangerous ride bound for collision. Her mission was clear. She was going to find the dagger.

A moment later, she found herself someplace she never wanted to see again. She willed herself to leave but her feet were heavy. As if sensing the conflict within, her body tensed. Waves of nausea rolled through her. The darkness rose, curling around her, its long tentacles taking hold.

"Much better," she said, her voice deeper than normal.

A line of frost extended across the floor, reflecting the light of the moon from the window. She stepped forward awkwardly, her legs wobbly. When the frost reached the door, it ran up the wood, covering it completely. As it continued to spread to the wall it burst into flames, devouring the door before disappearing. She stepped over the remnants and found herself in a long hall.

The memories of the last time she had been in Medora

flooded her. She was herself, but not. All the memories were hers, although they were distorted, twisted around the darkness within her.

A man in a long black robe appeared to her left. He cocked his head when he saw her, trying to place who she was and what she wanted. A moment later, recognition dawned on his face. Lana didn't give him a chance to say anything.

"The dagger, where is it?"

His eyes narrowed. "How do you know about that?"

The voices in her head grew louder, consuming her once more. She placed her hands on her forehead and pushed, trying to silence them. She screamed, the voices warping her thoughts, keeping her from thinking clearly. The man inched backward before turning around and running down the hall.

His footsteps echoed, and she concentrated on the sound, pushing the voices away. With a flick of her wrist the man stopped running. He fell, his hands slapping against the floor. She slowly walked forward as the man slid back to her. She placed her foot on top of his back.

"Where is it?"

He tried to stand. He panted for breath, clawing at the floor. She looked up at the sound of a door closing. It had come from downstairs.

"Help!" the man called.

Lana pushed her foot harder on his back. The frost reached his feet and quickly spread, covering him completely. When his screams grew silent, she stepped away, the thin line of frost following. When she came to the stairwell it pooled at her feet, forming a circle around her, wanting to protect her. She wrapped her fingers around the railing, surprised to find it cold. The frost crept down the stairs, leading the way. When she reached the first floor, she paused, listening for any indication where everyone was—where Alderic was.

As the line spread, she stepped off the staircase and

followed it. She walked slowly, stopping only when the frost ran underneath a large double door. Her eyes ran over the wood, looking at the engravings. A memory bubbled to the surface, rising above the crowded voices in her head. She had been here before. She remembered being terrified, fearing for her life. The funny thing was, she was no longer afraid.

Lana held her arm out, tracing the engraved wood with her fingertips. The dark energy of the room surrounded her, drawn to her. With a wave of her hand the door opened, inviting her in. The frost circled around her feet as she stepped inside.

Through the large window, she saw the night sky speckled with stars. The frost snaked its way through the empty room, climbing the walls. As she watched, the memories came. She walked to the table and sat in the same chair she had the last time she had been there. As the frost covered the walls, the temperature in the room dipped and she saw her breath.

She placed her hands on the table, watching the thin line of frost cover the window, blanketing her in darkness. Where was everyone? Where was Alderic? What did he have over the Council? It was the only explanation. He had to have something on them. How had he escaped? Why wasn't the Council doing anything to find him? They said they had their best reapers searching for him, but it didn't make sense. Medora was the first place they should have searched. People had seen him, surely word had reached the Council.

As Lana made her way into the hall, the frost began melting. She closed the doors behind her when she heard voices.

"We need more. What have you been doing down there?"

Lana stepped into the shadows. Damon appeared in the small foyer. He was holding something in his hands, showing it to the woman next to him.

The woman bent her head. "We've been working through the night."

"You haven't—" Damon's voice stopped mid-sentence.

When she was sure time had frozen, Lana stepped into the hall. Damon and the woman had been walking toward her, both paused mid-stride. Damon's mouth was open, his eyes narrowed maliciously at the woman next to him. He held his right arm out and the woman's eyes were trained on the object in the palm of his hand.

Lana followed the line of frost as it made its way toward her cousin. She plucked the object out of his palm. She held it up, studying the brassy yellow rock. Even in the dark hall she knew what it was. What was Damon doing with gold?

Lana left her cousin and made her way downstairs. The discovery was lodged in her head, and she tried to make sense of it. Were they digging for gold in the caves? What were they doing with it? Damon said they needed more. For what?

At the end of the staircase, she opened the door that led to the caverns. The air was heavy, and the ground was wet. When the frost extended, meeting the damp earth, it froze in slick patches. She heard voices and strained her ears, trying to hear over the sound of the river.

Lana clamped her hand around the gold, holding it tight. She stepped away from the water and hid in the shadows, ducking between the stalagmites and boulders. A group of rebels were near the river's edge. When their shovels hit the ground they knelt, as if examining the dirt.

"I knew you would come back to me."

Lana circled toward the voice. Her excitement rose, the thrill of confrontation in the air. She crossed her arms over her chest when a spark of light lit up the area before her, revealing Alderic.

"Just who I wanted to see," she said. "Father of the year."

He pushed off the wall, stepping forward. "I must say, I'm surprised to see you so soon. I suppose I have you to thank for Alexander's escape?"

This was news to Lana. The last time she had been in

Medora, Terris gave Alexander a knife. Had he used it to escape? She stepped forward, her eyes searching the shadows for any threats.

"I don't know what you mean."

"Somehow he obtained a knife," Alderic said, his voice flat. "Right after you escaped. You're stubborn, just like your mother. It's no matter though, he won't survive long out there."

Lana uncrossed her arms. Alderic's eyes followed the movement. She held the gold out, his eyes widened in surprise.

"Now where did you get that?"

She tossed the gold into the air, catching it easily. Alderic's mouth turned down. He stepped forward, restraining himself from reaching for it.

"You're stealing from me now?"

"What are you doing down here? Mining for gold? To pay off your debts?" As the words came out of her mouth a realization hit her. "You're paying off the Council."

He dropped his arm, the light above his hand still floating. "When I heard what happened, I didn't think you'd survive. Look at you."

She tossed the gold in the air again. "What about me?"

He raised his eyebrow. "You're thriving, you're strong, exactly what I had hoped for."

The anger burned inside her. She clenched her fingers around the gold. She squeezed, the rage filling her. A million thoughts overtook her, taking space in her already cramped head. He couldn't be serious.

"The power, the magic inside of you is because of me," he continued.

The gold crumbled in her grip. She opened her palm, watching the fragments fall to the ground. A line of thick frost wound its way from her feet, devouring it.

Alderic laughed. "There's more where that came from. The caves are full of gold."

"Answer me," she demanded. "You're paying the Council off? That's how you escaped?"

Alderic clenched his jaw. "Do you really think Damon would have gotten me out if they weren't in on it?"

"You told Ramos it happened during your cell transfer?" Lana said, piecing together what he was dangling before her.

Alderic's eyes swept over hers. "That part was true. It did happen during my cell transfer. That the Council initiated."

Flashes of black crossed her vision. The demons fed off her undulating emotions. Her skin tingled and her fingers surged with power, the magic yearning for release. The frost extended further, marking a path between them.

"Come now, don't look so dismayed," he said. "You didn't actually think the Council was helping people, did you?" When she didn't answer, he chuckled. "They only look out for themselves. The thirteen families are easily bought. It took me longer than I liked, but a lifetime of gold and jewels wore them down, just as I knew it would."

Lana shouldn't have been surprised. The amount of wealth flaunted by the Council was staggering. When the looting began, the thirteen families had banded together, not to protect others, but to protect themselves, their assets. Years of power had corrupted them even more.

"I read an interesting letter earlier," she said, her eyes glazing over the rebels' excavation site. "It was from Amos, to Shandra."

He smirked. "That was a twist I didn't see coming. I hadn't expected her to be in Mt. Sinclair, working with *him*. If you hadn't killed her, I would have."

"Why didn't you free him? You left him in the Yards?"

Alderic's lips curled. "The deal was for me. Why would I help Amos when he wants to harm you? All the work I did for you, and he wants to undo it."

Lana's eyes met his again. "Where's the dagger?"

"Dagger?" he asked, shaking his head subtly. "I have a lot of daggers. You need to be more specific."

On reflex, she raised her arm, and he flew backward. He hit the wall, jagged pieces of rock digging into his back. A twisted grimace contorted his face and his eyes danced with a rage all their own.

"You forget your place," he snarled. "I'm your father."

A tall rebel joined them, having heard the commotion. Alderic held his hand up, silently motioning for him to stay where he was, his eyes not leaving Lana for a second.

"Amos learned of the dagger years ago," he answered, still struggling against the magic. "When King Mathias called them into our world, he came to regret it. He cared too much. He had an opportunity of a lifetime and he wasted it. The point of all good mentors is that we get to learn from them, rise above their mistakes."

"The dagger?" she said, her mouth tight.

"Release me from your hold first."

She held his gaze. He struggled against the magic, trying to free himself. Her need for answers overpowered her need for revenge. She looked away, releasing him from the spell and he fell to the ground.

"Where is it?" Lana asked. "Is it here? In the caves?"

Alderic shrugged. "I haven't found it yet. It may not even be here."

That was good news. At least she had a chance to find it before he did. The demons shrieked in her ears.

"Why do you want it?" he asked.

Lana's eyes locked on his. She hated that she had his eyes. They were the same size, shape, and color.

"I'm sending them back."

He laughed, the sound echoing. "Now why would you do that?" When she didn't answer, he continued, "Don't believe their lies."

The frost continued forward. Lana watched it make its way closer to Alderic, imagining it overtaking him, covering him.

"We want the same thing." She paced forward.

"What would that be? Control? Power?"

Lana's skin tingled, the voices in her head rising. "For them to be sent home."

Another smile crept upon his face, pushing his gaunt cheekbones higher. "Is that what they told you? It's a lie. They're controlling you already. They want to be here."

"And how would you know what they want?"

"Common sense," he said. "All the people to feed on. Why would they want to leave? There's a reason I called on them."

Lana was quiet. It didn't matter what he said. She would never trust him anyway. She needed the dagger. Obviously, it wasn't in the caves. Alderic would have found it by now.

"I'm doing this for us," he added. "With the dagger, I can release them from you. You won't have to die. No one will. The dagger's shrouded in sacrificial magic. The final piece to releasing them. They'll obey me, I can control them."

"You're not doing this for us," she said, grinding her teeth.

He shifted on his feet, his long dark robe camouflaging him. "You're my daughter. Everything I did was for you. I miss Kalinia every day. A part of her lives on in you."

Lana hadn't been expecting that. He frowned, lost in the memories of his wife. His breathing slow, shallow. She almost felt bad for him. He lost Kalinia so young. But nothing would make her forgive him.

"I'll never be okay with what you did."

His gaze drifted to his feet. "When you're a parent you'll understand the need to protect your child at all costs. I was only making you strong. Help me find it and we'll control them...together."

Lana closed her eyes. Her skin vibrated, making it hard to

concentrate. She pushed his voice out of her head, focusing instead on her breathing, trying to remain calm.

"I'm fixing everything you did to me," she said, her voice a whisper. "I'm giving Terris his magic back, I'm sending them back, to their land."

Alderic's thin lips curled up. "There it is. Their plan. The weaker you are, the easier you'll be to subdue. They're playing you. Give the boy his magic back, you're only making it easier for them."

"I control them now," she said, opening her eyes.

Alderic laughed, the sound echoing over the steady flow of water. "No. You may have some control, but its temporary. They haven't cracked you yet."

Rage flashed through her. She clenched her fists.

"There may be a part of you holding on, clinging to yourself but it won't last. It won't be long before they completely over-power you. They'll get you to release them. They know you aren't strong enough to control them. Soon, they'll be free to do as they please and you'll be too weak to stop them."

Strong hands gripped her from behind. Two more rebels had joined them. When she was subdued, Alderic stepped forward confidently. He smiled, baring his teeth.

"I'll always have your best interests at heart."

Lana's blood boiled. His arrogance was maddening. The dark magic inside her yearned to be released. Her skin grew hot, beads of sweat dripping down her face. The rebels holding her screamed in pain. They released her, holding their hands out, revealing large blisters. Their skin red and raw. She turned to the man to her right as he fell to the ground. His screams invigorated her, giving her life.

She snapped her head back to Alderic. A blood curdling scream escaped her lips. She raised her arms and two balls of fire appeared above her palms, floating in the air.

"This is all your fault," she said between clenched teeth. "Everything wrong in my life stems from you."

Alderic's eyes followed the balls of fire above her palms. She launched them forward. The frost spread again, covering everything in its path. It devoured the rebels on the ground, their screams barely audible over the wind.

Alderic dashed to his right, barely missing the balls of fire. He ran toward the door. She smiled wide, the demons growing stronger, eager for more. With one last look at the destruction around her, Lana disappeared, dissolving into the darkness.

## 12

# THE BARRIER BETWEEN

The ground beneath her feet was hard, slick with dew. She opened her eyes and found herself in the one place she knew she could cause the most destruction. She fed off the feeling. The power was intoxicating.

The leaves shook in the cold breeze as she stepped out of the line of trees into the moonlight, the lake coming into view. The water was calm. For a moment, her heart rate increased as flashes of her time in Altaris came to mind. She remembered being captured by the Altarians. She remembered being their prisoner. She remembered Queen Gwendolyn leaving her to die in the underwater cave.

The memories came fast and furious, overwhelming her. What would happen when the demons had complete control? Would they push her away? Would she lose her memories? Would she cease to exist?

Realizing she was overcoming their hold, the demons pushed even harder. A sharp, throbbing pain pierced her forehead. Her stomach coiled as hot bile rose, burning her throat, spilling onto her lips. She fell to the ground and pushed out a scream, hoping it would alleviate the pain.

Another gust of wind wrapped around her. When the breeze settled, and the leaves stilled, her gaze fell on the lake once more. She stood, drawn to the underwater world and its inhabitants.

When she was at the water's edge, she scanned the forest. All was quiet. The Altarians were nowhere to be seen. A yellow fish popped its head above the water and small ripples broke the smooth surface. Lana looked for the spot she had almost drowned. Queen Gwendolyn was building a barrier to one day separate her city from the outside world. She was going to break it.

As the fish disappeared, Lana noticed that the left side of the lake was duller than the right. She was surprised at how fast it was spreading. Lana kicked off her shoes and removed her cloak. The water was cool on her skin. Tiny goosebumps dotted her arms. With each passing shiver, she grew even more determined. She wanted her revenge. Swimming in their lake would bring them to the surface.

Once she reached the opposite bank, she circled around, leisurely making her way to the middle. She swam on her back, letting herself loose to float, carefully avoiding the barrier. She closed her eyes. When she heard movement below, she swam to her belongings. A slimy fin brushed past her leg as tiny bubbles rose all around her.

Back on land, her gown was heavy, clinging to her skin. She draped her cloak over her shoulders as the Altarians surfaced. She watched their bodies dry quickly, the water seeming to evaporate before her eyes. The man closest to her gasped for breath as two slits on either side of his neck disappeared, sinking into his slick skin. Once the gills vanished, he sucked in a mouthful of air and spun around to face Lana. His eyes narrowed as he focused on her, tracking her every movement.

All around, the rest of the Altarians took their first breaths. They surrounded her as another splash of water drew her attention. Queen Gwendolyn swam to the edge of the lake. Her pale-yellow eyes searched Lana's. Her gills disappeared into her skin. She pushed her long gray-green hair off of her shoulder.

"You're very brave to come back."

Lana didn't say anything. The Altarians were silent, waiting for instructions from their queen. Droplets of water coursed down their bodies, the noise grating her nerves. Queen Gwendolyn stepped forward shakily. Her legs not used to walking on land. A man next to her reached out, supporting her from falling.

Lana watched the queen struggle. "Walk much?"

Queen Gwendolyn regained her balance. Her soldiers closed ranks. They surrounded her, ready to fight.

"There's something different about you," Queen Gwendolyn said, just loud enough for Lana to hear. "The magic is stronger. You've joined your father."

Lana chuckled. The idea was absurd. Why would she join Alderic? Why would she join his Rebellion? She was stronger than him, stronger than he would ever be. There was no reason to join him.

"Why are you here?" Queen Gwendolyn continued when Lana didn't answer. "Have you come to poison us again?"

Lana clicked her tongue, enunciating each word. "I never poisoned you."

"No." Gwendolyn sighed. "You didn't, but your father did. I can see that you've changed. You're not the same meek little girl that was here before. I can think of only one thing you would come back for. Revenge."

"Revenge?" Lana asked, her head cocked to the side. "What would make you say that?"

Queen Gwendolyn's eyes met hers again. "For killing Gavril. For trying to kill you."

Lana smiled. She did want revenge, and this was the perfect opportunity for it. While she had never met her Uncle Gavril, she knew the Rebellion may not have even happened if he were still alive. She took a moment to ponder what her life would have been like if she hadn't needed to go into hiding. Kalinia would still be alive, and she would have been raised in Bridian with both of her parents. Alderic may not have spiraled. He may not have gone to the Revatto. He may not have called forth the demons.

"It doesn't matter though," the queen said, interrupting her thoughts. She whirled around and addressed her subjects, "Kill her."

Two men stepped forward from the forest, piercing the circle of soldiers. They pointed their bows at Lana. She heard the release of arrows and faced them head on. She held her right hand out and watched the arrows fall to the ground. The Altarians let out a collective gasp.

"How did you do that?" Queen Gwendolyn asked, her eyes wide.

Lana didn't answer her question, instead saying, "Care to try again?"

She wasn't sure how she knew they were coming but spun around to see a barrage of arrows flying toward her. She held up both hands and imagined the arrows falling to the wet ground. A moment later, they stopped in midair. She felt stronger than she had before. Almost as if she were one with the dark magic.

Lana looked at the lake. There was one last thing she had to do before she left. She teleported across the water, to the other side. When she was near the barrier, she knelt down and touched it. Her hands slid across the slimy surface. She focused her energy on her palms and felt them warming the barrier. It dissolved, sinking to meet the underwater castle. Lana met Queen Gwendolyn's gaze.

"You should have killed me when you had the chance."

Before she could reply, Lana swiveled and ran into the

forest. She heard the muffled cries of the Altarians and relished the sound. Her heart hammered in her chest and the adrenaline coursed through her body. She wasn't sure where she was going to go but knew one thing for certain: she had never felt more alive and couldn't imagine going back to her previous life.

Lana ran until the sun rose. She hadn't stopped, there had been no need. She was fueled by their anger, fear, and confusion. The thought that she would go back when they least expected it invigorated her. A flash of black crossed her path and she stopped, looking for the source of the shadow.

A chorus of pops exploded around her. Half a dozen Shadow Splinters appeared before her, sniffing the air, trying to find Lana in their daze. The huge wolf-like creatures walked on their hind legs, their long black cloaks billowing in the wind as their beady yellow eyes blindly searched for her shadow. Thick black smoke filled the forest as they teleported all around her.

A loud pop sounded behind her and she twisted around to see a Shadow Splinter inches from her. Its long, sharp teeth snapped wildly in the air as it went on all fours, sniffing the ground. A flock of birds took flight from a nearby tree. She was no longer scared. All she wanted was to put them in their place.

The beast stood, reaching its furry hand toward her, stopping inches from her face. She had been discovered but didn't care. The Shadow Splinter grabbed her wrist and let out a long ear-piercing howl.

As the others closed in, she focused her energy into her hands and the Shadow Splinter howled in pain. It released her and fell to the ground. The others rushed toward her, and she held up her arms, palms out, creating an invisible barrier they couldn't penetrate. They sensed her power and stepped back, away from her. As one, they lowered their heads, as if in prayer.

"Do you see how much better life can be with us?"

She was surprised to see the demon leaning against a tree. He stood, brushing the dark hair off his face, his other hand wrapped around a small branch. He pulled it from the tree and snapped it in half. Somewhere deep down, Lana felt a stirring deep in her belly. The sight of the demon took her back to the Council's chambers. She looked up, her former self clawing to be released.

"What's happening to me?"

He smiled. "You just won't give in."

Lana looked around, struggling out of her trance. Flashes of the forest assaulted her, replaced with the memories of meeting the Council members and finding Amos's letter. She remembered losing control in front of the Council. She remembered the look on her uncle's face. What was she going to do? How was she going to fix this?

On cue, the memories of Altaris overtook her. She broke their barrier. Queen Gwendolyn had wanted her dead before. What was she going to do now? She stepped back, her foot slipping on a jagged rock. She caught her balance, but not before the demon let out a small chuckle.

"Let me go," she said. "I'll look for the dagger. I don't want this."

His gaze drifted. "Aren't you enjoying this? Don't you enjoy the power?"

Lana instinctively took another step backward, trying to put as much distance between them as she could. Her mouth ran dry, she couldn't even answer if she wanted to. She shook her head, fighting for control.

"I brought you back to tell you that we're going to find the dagger. You keep fighting us and it's distracting. Just let us in, give us full control. The sooner you let us find it, the sooner you'll be free. It's a win-win situation."

Lana didn't believe him. It couldn't be that easy. She moved further away from him, her legs trembling.

"What did you do to me?" she asked. "How were you able to control me? I would never do any of this on my own."

He stepped forward. "That means we almost have you."

"Stop!" Lana said, holding her hands out in front of her. "Stay away from me."

He smiled but stopped walking. His head tilted slightly to the left, watching her, waiting to see what she would do.

"How were you able to overpower me so easily this time? What changed?"

The demon opened his mouth and exhaled loudly; the movement exaggerated. His eyes met hers again and he said, "We're getting stronger. We're no longer fighting among ourselves. When we work together, it's easier to overpower you, make you do what we want." He stuck his tongue out, running it across his lips. "All the turmoil you caused back there was delicious, exactly what we needed."

Lana's eyes met his. "Please. Don't do this."

Her body shook, shaking off his wrath. Her own anger flashed through her, and the frost appeared, creating a small circle around her. The vivid green grass was now coated in the thin white frost. She tried to control it, to send it toward the demon but it remained by her feet.

"Let us find it." He stepped forward again. "Let us do what we need to do and have a bit of fun while we're at it. We want the same thing. Stop fighting."

Lana shook her head. A part of her wanted to give in. To let the demons shoulder the burden of finding the dagger. Another part of her couldn't believe her thoughts. She couldn't give into them. Even if they kept their word that she would be free, she didn't know what they had planned. Was Alderic right? Did they only want their freedom with no intention of returning to their land?

"No," Lana said. "I'll keep fighting."

He crossed his arms over his chest. "We're so much more powerful than you. We want our freedom back. We want our lives back. For the time being, just admit that you enjoy it."

Lana tensed at the thought. She did enjoy the power, the feeling that she could do anything. She hated to admit it, but there was a small part of her that didn't want to fight. She didn't have to be scared anymore. With the demons, she didn't have to fear Alderic or the Council. But if she did what he asked, gave them full control of her body, her mind, what would happen to her?

The crunch of leaves broke the silence. She turned, expecting to see the Shadow Splinters. Instead, Angelica appeared behind her. Her glossy eyes were trained on her. What was she doing? Where were the Outcasts? Could she see the demon?

Something pierced Lana's calf. The pain radiated up her leg. She let out a small cry of surprise. Angelica stepped back as a warmth spread up Lana's leg. The realization hit her hard. What had Angelica injected into her? The demon disappeared into a cloud of black smoke. Lines of ice-blue frost spread, covering the grass around her before erupting in bright violet flames.

**13**

———

# THE DARKEST NIGHT

Lana dreamed of fire. It was dark, destructive...beautiful. It called to her, beckoning her within its harsh reach. The violet flames were blinding. Small particles of bright ash floated into the air. Her muscles tensed, aching to reach for them.

She had been standing in a field of wildflowers. The bright green, vivid blues, and pale yellow in stark contrast to the dusk skyline. The fire devoured everything in its path, spreading from flower to flower, jumping from each petal. She watched, unable to move.

A wolf howled and she startled awake. Darkness greeted her. Her calf muscles ached, and she rolled over onto her back. Her eyes adjusted to the lack of light. She strained her ears, hoping to hear if anyone was nearby.

"Don't move," a childlike voice said. "You need to give the Ondebell time to leave your system."

Lana pivoted toward the voice. Angelica was next to her, sitting with her back against a tree trunk, her small legs spread out. Her porcelain face staring into the forest.

"What happened?" Lana croaked.

"The Ondebell knocked you out," Angelica answered.

Lana couldn't make sense of her answer. What was Ondebell? She rolled over again, her back on the ground, listening to the wind. Angelica stood and slowly made her way to Lana. She held out a clear bottle.

"What's that?"

"Water."

Lana sat, her stomach churning. She opened the container and drank. The cold liquid slid down her throat. She was so thirsty she drank the entire bottle.

Her calf cramped again, sending shockwaves of memories through her. Angelica injected something into the muscle. What was it? Some kind of poison? What would it do to her? Would she be all right?

"Did you poison me?"

"No," Angelica answered. "Well, maybe a little. You'll be fine."

Streaks of pink and orange lit up the dark sky. Angelica placed the bottle into a bag at her feet while Lana watched the sun slowly rise, chasing away the night.

"Where are they?" she asked. "The Outcasts?"

Angelica shrugged. "They told me where to find you. They gave me the Ondebell, told me to use it on you."

The feeling in her legs came back and she stretched. The charm on her bracelet dangled off her wrist and she placed a hand on her chest, sighing with relief when she felt the necklace. Even though she was happy that she hadn't lost them, she was unsettled. It felt as if something big was coming, something she couldn't escape. Her head was clear, the demons subdued for the time being. She should be happy.

"The Outcasts are still tracking me?"

Angelica nodded. "How do you feel?"

Lana was unsure how to answer. Her mouth was dry. She swallowed, feeling the saliva glide down her throat. She looked around her surroundings, hoping to find something else to drink when she remembered Altaris. She broke their barrier. How many years had it taken to create for her to obliterate it in only a moment? Her frantic thoughts shifted to the Council.

"What do I do?"

Angelica looked away. "What we all do. Continue on. Move forward with the knowledge that everyone is fighting something."

Lana sighed. She didn't understand. Angelica didn't have the demons inside her. She didn't have powers that she couldn't control. She looked up, about to explain that her situation was different when Angelica touched her arm, the cool porcelain startling against Lana's warm skin.

"I'm sorry," Lana said. "I didn't mean to put this on you. I know that you have it worse. You've been trapped inside this doll. It's not right. It's not fair."

Anger seeped into her, igniting the flame deep in her belly. It hadn't been fair that Angelica was now relegated to living inside a doll. She wished she could do something to make it right.

"It's not about who has it worse," Angelica said. "It's about making it right. Helping others, even when you don't feel—"

An arrow flew by them, hitting a tree. Lana spun just in time to see another hit the back of her shoulder. When it made contact, she screamed. The arrow sliced her skin before dropping to the ground. The pain radiated outward, dulled by shock. What was happening? Who was attacking them?

More arrows flew by their heads. Lana ducked and reached for Angelica. She closed her eyes, willing them somewhere else, somewhere safe. When nothing happened, she stood. With Angelica still in her arms she began running, skirting around large trees, and dodging the barrage of arrows.

"What's happening?" she asked, panting for breath.

"Altarians," Angelica answered. "They've been following

you. I was hoping we'd be gone by the time they made it this way."

Lana jumped over a fallen tree branch. Her shoes weren't made for running. They were tight and wet, the straps digging into her skin. They were made for appearances only, not running for your life.

"Watch out!" Angelica said, pointing to her right.

Out of the corner of her eyes, Lana saw a man running toward them. She turned to get a better look, her stomach sinking when she saw the Altarian. He had almost reached them. Her heart hammered in her chest. They were about to be caught and there was nothing she could do. She didn't know why she had been unable to teleport. It didn't make sense. Her calf muscle cramped again, and it hit her. The poison. What-ever Angelica had injected into her was inhibiting her magic.

The man reached for Lana, his fingers brushing up against her. She forced herself to keep running, to pick up her pace. Her legs ached and her shoulder screamed in agony, but she didn't stop. She knew she didn't have long.

As the Altarian lunged forward, she sidestepped him, turning to the left. In her haste, her right foot caught on an exposed tree root, and she fell. Angelica tumbled out of her arms. Lana crawled to her, knowing she only had a few moments before the Altarian would reach them. She threw her hand on Angelica's leg and closed her eyes, willing her body to teleport with everything she had left. She felt the subtle shift and knew it had worked.

"What happened?" Angelica asked. "Where are we?"

Lana opened her eyes. They were on the floor. She looked up, surprised to see that she was at Emeric's, in his living room. The room was dark, empty, and cold. She stood, the pain in her shoulder overwhelming.

"Somewhere safe," she answered, helping Angelica stand.

Footsteps echoed in the hall. Lana got up just in time to see her cousins run into the room. Deliah stopped when she saw them, her eyes wide. Dominic ran into his sister. Terris followed behind them. When he saw her, he too stopped walking.

Dominic's eyes lit up when he saw Lana. "Where have you been? What happened to you?"

Before Lana had a chance to answer, Deliah stepped forward, looking at Angelica. "Where have you been? Lana, where'd you find her?"

Dominic rolled his eyes when he saw Angelica. "Great."

Angelica brushed herself off. "It's nice to see you too."

Lana didn't have time for their questions. She had more important things to worry about. "Where is everyone? My parents? Ramos?"

"Right here," Jacqueline said from the doorway, her hands covering her mouth in disbelief over what she was seeing, that Lana was really there.

Lana ran to her. She wrapped her arms around her waist as Jacqueline squeezed her tight, afraid she would disappear again.

"You're bleeding," Grayson said.

Lana wiggled out of Jacqueline's embrace. Now that her attention had been brought back to it, her shoulder ached. Before she could answer, Ramos and Emeric joined them from the hallway.

Lana couldn't look at her uncle, she was embarrassed. She had let the demons win. She had let them overpower her, once again. Grayson placed his hands on her back to study the wound. He brushed her hair away and leaned over.

"What happened?" he asked, his eyes darting from Lana to Angelica. "Were you hit with an arrow?"

Lana was quiet. She used the time to think of an answer. How was she supposed to tell them what she had done? How was she supposed to tell them that the Altarians were now hunting her? How was she supposed to live with the guilt?

"Altarians," Angelica answered.

"I need to find the dagger," Lana interrupted.

She was running out of time. The demons were winning, slowly intertwining themselves with her, controlling her thoughts and her actions. Her priority should be finding the dagger before it was too late, before the demons overtook her or the Altarians exacted their revenge.

Grayson crossed his arms over his chest. "What dagger? You need to have your shoulder looked at. It might be infected."

Lana shook her head. "No. There's no time. I did something, something terrible. Now the Altarians are angry. I don't think I have much time. I need to get them out of me. Then I can focus on repairing relationships, letting the Council know that I'm no longer a danger, letting the Altarians know it wasn't really me."

Jacqueline's eyebrows furrowed and she held up her hand. "Slow down. Let's start at the beginning. What dagger? What happened to the Altarians? Why did you leave the Council Ball?"

"There isn't much time," Ramos interrupted. "I assume reapers are already searching for you."

Lana's stomach dropped. Everything around her began spinning. Even though her feet were steady, the chaos around her was too much to bear. What did he mean? Had the Council made the decision to send her to the Yards?

Jacqueline took Lana's hand. "It's going to be okay. Now that you're here, you're safe. Grayson and I will leave with you. We won't let them find you."

Lana turned to Ramos. "Are they going to send me to the Yards?"

He sighed. "After you left, they held an emergency meeting. They decided that you're too unpredictable, too dangerous. They held a vote and unanimously agreed to send you to the Yards. Until another solution can be found."

Her mouth ran dry. Her hands flew to her chest, trying to

steady her frantic breathing. Her shoulder ached, the pain radiating outward into her neck, but she couldn't focus on that. She couldn't focus on anything.

"Jacqueline and I were going to look for you," Grayson said. "We'll run. There are places they won't find us."

"She looks fine to me," Dominic said. "Why are they doing this? Why are they sending her to the Yards?"

Deliah took her brother's hand. Ramos looked at his children.

"It'll be okay," he said.

"No," Lana said. "It won't be. The Council isn't helping. All they care about is protecting themselves. They let Alderic escape. He bribed them."

Everyone was quiet as they processed her outburst. Lana used their silence to look around the room. It appeared exactly as it had the last time she had been there. Then she realized that it hadn't been that long, only two days. But to her it seemed as if an entire lifetime had passed.

"Why would you say that?" Ramos asked. "You can't make up stories about them."

"We don't have time for this," Jacqueline said. "We have to leave. The sooner we do, the greater our chances of evading the reapers."

Emeric disappeared into the hall. Everyone was quiet again, all eyes on her. Lana felt sick. How had this happened? How had this become her life?

She inhaled deeply. "I found a letter from Amos. It was written to Shandra. He mentioned a dagger. I need to find it."

"Lana, slow down," Grayson said, his face etched with worry.

"No." Lana stepped back, away from everyone. "I need to find it. If I do, I can send them back, everything will go back to normal."

"How will a dagger help?" Deliah asked, still clutching her brother's hand tightly.

Lana sighed. Were they even listening to her? "It will release them."

"Start over," Ramos said. "What dagger?"

Lana pinched the bridge of her nose, the words spilling out. "When King Mathias released the demons, he realized his mistake. He killed himself with the same dagger that was used in the sacrifice. It will release them. The Revatto knew the power it held and hid it."

Lana knew she wasn't making sense. She was talking too fast for anyone to follow.

"In Medora?" Terris asked, seeming to read her train of thoughts. "Is that what they were doing in the caves?"

Lana nodded. "They're still looking for it. They're also mining for gold. Alderic is paying them off. That's how he escaped."

"Paying who off?" Ramos said. "Lana, we're in over our heads. We don't know what to do. The Council will help. They only want to isolate you until we have a solution. It's not ideal but it's the best they can come up with. They're not the bad guys here."

Lana turned on him. "They may not be the bad guys, but they're part of the problem. They let him escape." She turned to Terris. "Tell them, tell them that they were digging, mining for something when we were in Medora."

"They were," Terris answered. "But why does he want the dagger now? Doesn't he know that you already broke the Crystal?"

"Yes," she said. "Will everyone just listen to me? The dagger will release them. Whoever releases them can send them back or control them. I can't let Alderic find it."

Grayson nodded, trying to follow everything she was saying. "How do you know this? How did you find Angelica?"

"I found her," Angelica answered. "We've been tracking her."

No one asked for clarification. Everything Lana was saying had been confusing enough.

"What did you do to the Altarians?" Ramos asked, his voice grave. "Why did they attack you?"

Lana's stomach plummeted. An ice-cold chill curled around her, and she wrapped her arms around her chest, her shoulder aching. She didn't want to answer him. She didn't want to admit to it.

"If we're going to fix this, I need to know," Ramos said.

Lana bit her lip. All she wanted to do was fix it, mend her mistakes. Would it even be possible?

"Queen Gwendolyn had been building a barrier." She swallowed, buying a moment to build up the courage to finish. "I broke it."

The room was silent, everyone was trying to process what she had said. Terris averted his gaze from Lana. She could only imagine what her friend thought of her. Jacqueline took Grayson's hand.

Ramos finally broke the tension. "They've been building that barrier for years. How did you do it?"

Again, Lana didn't answer. She looked at the floor, too ashamed to say what they already knew.

"I found her right after," Angelica said. "I had Ondebell. It was enough to subdue them, for her to break free from the demons."

"I didn't mean to do it," Lana said. "I didn't mean for any of this to happen."

Now that her family knew everything, she felt lighter, like a weight had been lifted. Even though she had left out the small detail of seeing the demon. What would they make of that?

"Okay," Jacqueline said, her eyes darting around the room. "The first thing we have to do is get ready to leave."

"And look at your shoulder," Grayson said. "Emeric might have something we can put on it."

Ramos sighed. "The sooner you leave, the better."

Deliah dropped her brother's hand and looked at Lana. "I'm going to miss you."

Lana's eyes darted from Deliah, to Dominic, and landed on Terris. She was going to miss them. Hot tears sprang to her eyes, and she wiped them away. Her legs grew weak, and she sat on the couch, sinking into the cushion. Jacqueline and Grayson made to leave, and Deliah sat next to her, embracing her.

Grayson stopped, and said, "I'll be right back. I'm going to see what medication Emeric has."

"I'll go with you," Ramos said. He said to Angelica, "Are you okay for the time being?"

She nodded. "They'll find me."

Lana leaned into the seat of the couch, flinching when her shoulder hit the back. She looked at her cousins and Terris, wondering when she would see them again. She wished she could see Trevor and Ava one last time. Would she spend the rest of her life on the run from the Council? Would Grayson and Jacqueline spend the rest of their lives on the run? She thought of Grayson's brothers and a pit formed in her stomach. He may never see them again.

"You're getting blood on the couch," Deliah said, moving away from Lana. "Does it hurt?"

A pained scream echoed from the kitchen. Lana's breath caught in her throat. Against her better judgment, Deliah ran into the hallway. Dominic chased after her. Terris and Angelica looked at Lana, waiting to see what she was going to do.

As silence filled the house, Lana ran to the empty hall, listening for any other sounds. It was eerily quiet. Were the Altarians here? She knew it would take them a while to walk to Ganyon Falls, and how would they even know she was there? Was it the Council? Reapers? A part of her wanted to teleport but she couldn't leave her family without making sure they were all right.

"Let me go first," Terris whispered when they reached the kitchen door.

Lana shook her head. She didn't want anything to happen to him. Her heart thundered in her chest. Just when she thought she could relax, take a moment to gather her thoughts, something had to happen. What were the chances? Her cousins hadn't reappeared, the house was too silent.

Terris held his arm out, preventing her from going into the kitchen. She tried pushing him out of the way, but he had already begun moving to peek inside the door. If she miscalculated, if there was a threat inside the room, she didn't want to take the chance of him being seen because she pushed him out of the way.

"Hello, Lana," a cold voice sounded from behind, startling her.

Her blood ran cold. She slowly turned to face their guest. She didn't have time to teleport before the man reached out and took her arm.

**14**

---

# NOWHERE TO HIDE

Contlay held up a large knife, the blade glinting in the light. "I was hoping you would be here."

A woman stepped out of the kitchen. Her tight black pants hugged her legs, a stark contrast to the loose bright yellow shirt she was wearing. Long black hair fell down her back and her gray eyes narrowed at Lana.

"Tara." Contlay smiled. "Why don't you bring out our guest?" He said to Lana, "You'll want to stay for this. Heidi's been dying to see you again."

Lana was speechless. Did he say Heidi? Trevor's mom? Tara disappeared into the kitchen. A moment later she reappeared, dragging another woman out after her, her long arms around her captive's neck. It was Trevor's mom. Heidi stopped struggling when she saw Lana. Her face flushed and she nearly collapsed.

"Trevor?" Heidi whispered, tears streaming down her cheek. "Is he okay?"

Lana nodded. She ran to her, but Contlay stepped in her path. He took Heidi in his grasp, pushing Tara away. He held the knife against her throat, the blade drawing blood.

"He's fine," Lana whispered, her eyes darting back to Contlay. "What do you want? Let her go."

"I'll admit, she wasn't my first choice," he said. "I had been hoping for Ava or Trevor, but the timing worked out for Heidi."

Lana's head spun. Why did he want Ava or Trevor? What did he want to do with them? What was he planning to do with Heidi? This was the last thing she had been expecting.

He took another step closer to Lana and her breath hitched. The memories of his betrayal fresh. It still stung. She had grown up believing that he was on her side, protecting her.

"Why are you doing this? What are you going to do with her?"

He sighed. "I needed something to bring you back to Mt. Sinclair. I had the Crystal. I had a plan. Everything was set."

Heidi struggled for breath. She tried pushing herself out of his grip but wasn't strong enough. She was still in her scrubs and her face was dirty. She had been taken after work. Lana couldn't let anything happen to her. Trevor needed his mom.

"As always," Contlay continued. "You ruined that. You had to piece it together so quickly. I thought I had time. Then you went and broke the Crystal."

Lana's mind worked in overdrive, thinking of ways to keep him talking, to stall him so she could come up with a plan. She couldn't leave her family. She couldn't leave Heidi.

"How did you know I was here?"

Contlay cleared his throat. "As soon as I heard the reapers were looking for you, I knew I had to act fast. My contact in Bridian informed me that you weren't there, that you had gone to the Council Ball of all places. It made sense that you would all be here. I was prepared to wait it out, as long as I beat the Council and their reapers." His eyes darted back to hers. "You wouldn't have lasted long before they found you anyway. Be happy that I'm sparing you from the Yards."

The words stung. He was playing to her fear. Even though she knew what he was doing, it didn't make it any easier.

He tightened his grip on Heidi. "I'm only here to finish what I started."

Terris stepped closer to Lana, standing in front of Angelica, trying to shield them. Tara leaned against the doorframe, snapping a large piece of pink bubblegum between her lips.

"There's nothing to finish," Lana said.

Contlay didn't answer. Instead, he pointed to the kitchen door. When no one moved, he snapped, "In there."

Lana shook her head. It was too quiet in the kitchen. "What did you do with everyone? Where are my parents?"

His jaw locked and his eyes narrowed. "I asked you to go to the kitchen."

"And I asked you what you did with everyone?" Lana said, her voice rising.

Heidi gasped as Contlay dug the knife deeper into her neck. Her eyes pleaded with Lana to listen.

"What's the holdup?" Tara asked, popping the gum again.

Lana snapped at the woman. "Why are you helping him? He's evil."

Tara smiled. "I'm just in it for the money. My student loans are brutal."

Contlay raised his chin, puffing his chest. "In the kitchen, now, before I kill her and Trevor has to bury his mom."

Lana walked past Tara into the kitchen, her heart stopping at the scene before her. Ramos was sprawled on the floor, his eyes were closed and breathing stilled. Sitting at the table were Emeric, Grayson, and Jacqueline. Deliah and Dominic were huddled on the floor near their father. Scattered around the room were three other people, all with guns trained on her friends and family.

"Leave," Jacqueline said, looking at Lana, urging her to teleport.

"I wouldn't if I were you," Contlay warned. "I'll kill them all."

All eyes were on her, wondering what she would do. Angelica stepped closer, skirting between Lana and Terris. Lana brushed the hair off her face, trying to think clearly. The fear and confusion soaked the room, seeping into her. She inhaled deeply, letting it give her energy.

She asked Contlay again, keeping the fear and pleading out of her voice, "What do you want?"

"You know what I want," he said, his mouth twisted in a grimace.

Heidi shifted on her feet. Her hands moved to her throat, trying to pry Contlay's hands off. He snarled in response, pushing the knife deeper into the flesh. Heidi cried out in pain again, her legs trembling.

"You're too late," Lana said, hoping to draw his attention back to her. "I already broke it. What more could you want?"

"No," he snapped. "It's not too late. You may have put a dent in my original plan, but it's not over yet. If I kill you, they'll be released, and I'll control them."

Jacqueline gasped. Grayson slid his chair out. A tall man stepped in his path, pushing him back toward the table.

"They'll be sent back to their land if Lana dies," Emeric said. "Remember the stories of King Mathias?"

Contlay pointed to Terris. "That's where he comes in."

Terris held his hands out, as if shielding himself from the words. "What can I do?"

"You were both there that night," Contlay said. "You were both participants in the ceremony, albeit unwillingly, but that doesn't matter. If she dies, they'll be released and I have a theory that your magic, and the tether bond, will find its way back to you."

Lana listened with bated breath, trying to piece his theory together. Could it be true? Would his magic be returned?

Would he become the tether? The demon hadn't mentioned that possibility.

"That won't work," Lana said. "They told me if I die, they die. We need the dagger to release them. Let them go and I'll help you find it."

Even though it wasn't true, she would never help him, she wasn't above lying to keep her family safe.

"I can't believe you trust them." He snorted. "Although, you have a history of trusting the wrong people. And Shandra told me all about the dagger. She was adamant that it would release them from the Crystal. You already did that so there's no need for it, even if it did actually exist."

"You don't believe it's real?" Lana asked.

After a brief moment of consideration, Contlay answered, "I believe there was a dagger. I don't think it's as important as Amos thinks. I don't think it would have done anything to the Crystal." His eyes flickered from Lana to Terris. "Besides, there's been no trace of it. If it was really that important, the Revatto would have hidden it in the caves. I know Alderic's been looking for it. He has yet to find anything."

"He may be looking in the wrong place," Lana said. "I can help you find it. If we had it, it would release the demons, I would still be the tether. Someone will be able to control them. If you kill me, it'll just kill them."

Deep down, Lana knew it was true. There was a reason the demons hadn't killed her. It would have sealed their own fate.

"I still believe my theory," Contlay said, stepping forward. "We don't need you. Once I kill you, they'll be released, and your friend will be the tether. I'll be able to control them."

"Lana, go," Jacqueline called.

"Enough." Contlay held his hands out. "Mick, take care of her, all of them."

Lana's eyes widened. Time seemed to move in slow motion as the man behind Jacqueline aimed his gun at her. Jacqueline straightened her back, a lone tear sliding down her cheek. When she caught Lana's eye, she subtly nodded, letting her know to leave, to take who she could and flee.

Before Mick could pull the trigger, Lana did the one thing she knew would buy her a moment. Everyone froze. She hadn't been touching anyone, so she was by herself, alone with her thoughts. She looked away, thinking of a way out of the situation, a way where her family would stay safe.

"Quite the predicament."

Lana spun at the voice. The demon was standing next to Mick, studying the gun in his hands as if he had never seen anything like it before. He straightened, his black hair shining in the light.

"Leave me alone," she said, throwing her hands up in frustration.

Lana had more important things to worry about. How was she going to fix this?

Not one to be ignored, the demon said, "You know, we could have killed you by now. But I had been speaking the truth. You die, we die. Let us help."

Lana spun to face him. "I'm not myself when you're with me. Pain, confusion, fear...they keep me going...you going. That's the epitome of evil."

He looked out the window. "And pulling us from our home, not once but twice, isn't evil? Expecting us to behave a certain way, imprisoning us...all of that is fine?"

Lana's hand flew to her forehead. She didn't know if she was imagining him, if she was slowly losing her mind, but now wasn't the time for it. He went to Mick and placed his hand over the gun. A moment later, a thin layer of frost covered the barrel, rendering it useless.

"We want the same thing."

Before she could say anything, he disappeared. As if in slow motion, time restarted for everyone. Mick attempted to pull the trigger and let out a bloodcurdling scream when he realized his fingers were frozen inside the block of ice along with the gun.

"What happened?" Contlay asked, tossing Heidi toward Tara, and making his way toward Mick. "No one move," he added, his eyes darting across the room wildly.

Lana's eyes met Grayson's. His face was set, the determination clear. With Contlay focused on Mick's hand, he slid his chair back forcefully, knocking Contlay to the ground. Grayson had just enough time to tackle him before another man pulled him off.

Contlay stood and faced Grayson. He pulled his right hand past his waist, his fingers in a fist. When his hand collided with Grayson's cheek the room was silent. Grayson doubled over, blood dripping from his mouth.

Lana clenched her teeth. A low ringing echoed through her head, muting Contlay. A flash of black crossed her vision and she allowed it in.

When the ringing stopped, she trained her eyes on Contlay. He hadn't been paying attention to her, still taking his anger out on Grayson. She balled her fists, smiling when the frost covered the ground around her. Jacqueline jumped out of her chair. She threw herself on Contlay. They crashed to the floor, taking Mick with them.

"Do something," Tara said to the remaining two men.

Emeric stood and pushed one of them to the ground. The other advanced on Emeric, training his gun on him. Dominic took the opportunity to charge at the man. He fell forward, and his gun discharged. The bullet hit the wall, scattering chunks of plaster around them.

Tara's hands fell to her sides. "Do I have to do everything?"

As she made her way into the fray, Heidi lunged at her. Everyone was caught in the fighting, no one had even noticed the lines of frost slowly make their way outward, into the room.

"Go, now," Terris said.

Lana turned to her friend. He was bent low, talking to Angelica, urging her to leave, to hide, to look for help. Angelica looked up at Lana one last time before running to the door. Terris stood, his eyes darting across the room. When he noticed the frost, he gasped.

"What are you doing?"

The frost found its way to Tara first. It quickly covered her, freezing her in its grasp. Heidi managed to dodge the frost and jumped up with a scream. She backed away, watching it cover everything around her. Deliah and Dominic ran toward Terris.

"We have to go," Deliah said. "Now! We have to get help."

"I'm going to end this," Lana said.

Deliah grabbed Lana's hand, curling her fingers into hers. "This isn't you, Lana. Stop. Now's our chance to leave."

A gun fired, drawing their attention. More plaster rained down on them. When the dust settled, Contlay narrowed his eyes at Lana. He trained the gun in her direction, aiming at her. She didn't have time to react before he pulled the trigger.

# 15

# THE FINAL GOODBYE

Dominic pushed Lana out of the way. He stepped in front of her. Time moved in slow motion as the bullet pierced his stomach. His eyes met hers before he fell to the ground, blood pooling around him. Lana's hands flew to her mouth, an audible gasp escaping her lips, muted by Deliah's scream.

Contlay had the gun aimed at her. Jacqueline and Grayson were struggling with Mick. Emeric was kneeling on the floor next to Ramos, and Heidi was struggling with another of Contlay's men, preventing him from reaching Lana.

"Someone help him," Deliah screamed, her voice hoarse.

Lana heard the shot before she saw it. The bullet slowed before finally coming to a stop in midair. Deliah's screams quieted. The room was now silent, everyone frozen but her.

She ran to Dominic. Across from her, Deliah was holding her brother's hand. His mouth was flax, and his eyes were half-open, staring at the ceiling. Blood had pooled around him, an angry gash across his stomach.

"I need your help," Lana said, looking around the room frantically, hoping to find the demon.

She was met with silence. She looked at her cousin, willing

him to heal, hoping he would be okay. That it was all a horrible nightmare.

"Where are you?"

Lana's voice quivered. Where were the demons? Maybe they could help. She didn't even care what the price would be. She just wanted Dominic to be all right. She wanted her family to be okay.

"I'm right here," a quiet voice said.

Lana jumped. When she spun around, she saw Dominic. He was standing near the door. He looked happy, healthy. There was no blood. She ran to him, wrapping her arms around his neck. He chuckled but hugged her in return.

"I'm so glad you're okay." Dominic didn't say anything. She stepped back, narrowing her eyes at him. "You're okay, right?"

His eyes left hers, lingering on something behind her. She followed his gaze, and her heart sank. He was still laying on the floor, Deliah above him, holding his hand. The bright red blood circled around him.

"I don't understand."

He walked forward, stopping near Deliah. He bent down and placed his hand on her shoulder. He looked at his body. Lana couldn't bear to watch anymore and averted her eyes. When her gaze fell on Ramos, she couldn't stop the tears. She replayed the last moment before she had stopped time, wishing she could somehow reverse it. It happened so fast.

"Will you look after her for me?"

Lana made to see what Dominic was referring to and saw him watching his sister. She wanted to tell him to look after her himself. She wanted to tell him that he would be fine. She wanted to tell him everything would be all right. He would be all right. Instead, she said the only thing she could actually say, the only thing that was true in the moment.

"Yes."

Dominic's attention was caught by something to her right.

She followed his gaze but didn't see anything besides the door leading to the hallway. She was surprised to see a soft yellow light around him, almost as if it were coming out of him. His face lit up.

"What's happening?" Lana asked. "What are you looking at?"

"You don't see it?"

Lana followed his gaze again. When she still saw the door, she moved closer to him. Maybe the change in position would reveal what had caught his attention. She squinted, her eyes darting over everything in her peripheral vision. She didn't see anything out of the ordinary, anything that would hold his attention.

"I don't see anything."

He looked at her, a small smile on his face. "They're telling me you won't be able to see it. It's not time."

Lana's stomach clenched. Who was talking to him? It wasn't time for what? Nothing was making sense. Dominic's hands fell to his side, and he stepped forward. Lana reached out, taking his hand.

"What's happening?"

"I have to go," he said. "Tell my dad I love him. And my mom."

The light around Dominic grew so bright she had to look away. His arms wrapped around her. She sank into his embrace. At that moment, everything felt like it would be all right. He radiated comfort. The sugary-sweet smell of warm vanilla enveloped her. Another tear slid down her cheek and her legs buckled. As a fresh batch of tears fell down her face, she gripped her cousin tighter, as if that would keep him with her.

"It was always meant to be this way," Dominic said. "This is how it was always supposed to be. I did my part."

Lana wiped her face, but the tears kept coming. She didn't

understand. What was always meant to be? What was his part? Her eyes met his again. They were so bright, so full of life.

"I don't understand. What's happening? If you're dead, how am I talking to you? How can I see you?"

Maybe this was all a really bad dream. Maybe she would wake up in a moment. She closed her eyes, willing that when she reopened them, she would wake up from this nightmare.

"Lana," Dominic said. "This isn't a dream."

When she opened her eyes, Dominic was watching her with a serene smile on his face. She let her hands fall limply to her side. An audible cry escaped her, and she retreated again. When her back hit the wall, she slid down, placing her head in her hands.

"Your energy," Dominic said.

Lana looked up. Her eyes heavy, the effort to keep them open overwhelming her. The light around him dimmed. She kept her eyes on him, studying his features, hoping she wouldn't forget anything about him.

"They told me it's your energy," he continued. "You're vibrating higher than everyone else. That's why you can see me."

Lana pushed the hair out of her face. "Who told you? What does that even mean?"

"All of the magic," he said. "They're waiting for me."

Lana didn't understand. She would never understand magic and its consequences. She rubbed her eyes, trying to dry the tears blocking her vision. She sucked in a deep lungful of air.

"One day you'll understand." He smiled. "Don't let the darkness in."

With a sudden whoosh of air, Dominic disappeared. The bullet hit the wall. Deliah's sharp cry pierced Lana's ears again. Terris placed a comforting hand on Deliah's shoulder, his head whipping around, searching for something. When he saw

Lana, his face told her all she needed to know. It was true. Dominic was gone.

The frost slowly made its way through the room. The tall man swung his fist at Heidi, meeting her cheek and drawing blood. Heidi fell to the floor, her body weak. Contlay threw Grayson off of him. His body landed on the floor near Jacqueline, who was engaged in her own fight with Mick and the other man.

"Lana," Terris called. "Go."

For once, Lana was frozen. All around her, chaos ensued, and she couldn't move. Ramos sat up. Emeric helped him stand. He ran to his children, dodging the commotion around him. He cradled Dominic in his lap, his cry cutting her to the core.

Terris ran to Lana. He bent down, taking her hands, helping her stand. "You need to go. What are you doing?"

"I can't," she said, looking at him. "Dominic's dead because of me. This is all my fault. I need to do something."

The sharp fire of a gun rang out. Her hands flew to her ears too late, the loud echo reverberating, clouding her head. Her stomach twisted, bile rising. Across the room, she saw the demon. His hands were crossed over his chest, surveying the scene unfolding before him. His long body leaned against the wall; his feet crossed at the ankles. When he met her gaze, he winked.

A drop of blood fell on her lap, breaking the demon's spell over her. She was beginning to question if he was really there, if the man was real or just a figment of her imagination. Perhaps he was a manifestation, a vision she created to cope with the darkness around her. Another drop of blood fell into her lap. She ran her hands across her face trying to find the source of the blood, and realized it was coming from her nose.

Across the room, Contlay laughed as Grayson fell backward. When Grayson didn't move, Contlay kicked him, taunting him to stand. Jacqueline watched him being beaten; distracting her from her own fight. Mick used it to his advantage and swung hard, his fist connecting with her temple.

"There you are," Contlay said, looking at Lana. "We have unfinished business."

Contlay held up the gun, aiming it at her. The ringing in her head intensified. Terris grabbed her arm, trying to pull her down, out of the line of fire. In an instant, her head cleared, and she pushed Terris away.

As if in slow motion, Lana stepped forward. Contlay followed her movement, the gun still trained on her. Out of the corner of her eyes, Emeric stalked past Mick and the other man, their attention on Jacqueline who was now standing. Before Contlay had a chance to fire his weapon, Emeric jumped on him.

Jacqueline ducked as Mick threw another punch, barely missing his fist. He fell over. Contlay and Emeric wrestled for the gun.

"This is it, Lana," Terris said, his eyes darting around the room. "Now's your time to leave. Go. Hide from the Council."

"And leave you all to die?"

"He wants you," Terris said. "If you leave, if you're not here, he may go."

Deliah's cries brought her back. If she left, Contlay may follow her. He wanted her. Because of her, Dominic was dead. Because of her, Ramos lost a son and Deliah a brother.

Contlay was still struggling with Emeric, wrestling over the gun in his hands. Grayson was now standing, helping Jacqueline with Mick and his partner. Heidi was taking on the other man. If she left, she wouldn't see any of them again. She would never see her parents, her uncle, her cousin, her friends. Where would she even go? Then she realized it wouldn't even work. Contlay wouldn't stop if she left. If she disappeared, he would use her family and friends as collateral, as he had done with Heidi. He wouldn't give up so easily.

"Go," Lana whispered. "Find Angelica, help her."

"No," his face fell, realizing her plan. "You can't—"

Lana closed her eyes, envisioning the other side of the room, behind Contlay and Emeric. When she reopened them, she was in the spot she pictured. The demon had vanished.

Contlay swung his foot out, hitting Emeric's shin. Caught off guard, Emeric fell. Terris was the only one who noticed her move. He watched her for a moment before running to Deliah and Ramos. Lana focused her attention on Contlay.

The frost had stopped spreading. Lana held her arms out, envisioning it forming a circle around her and Contlay. The hair on the back of her neck stood on end and her arms tingled. As the frost wound its way back to her, she looked at Dominic's still body one last time.

When Ramos met her gaze, he stood. Deliah fell into Terris's arms. Lana nodded to her uncle. He seemed to understand what she was going to do and ran toward her, but the frost was faster. It built upon itself, creating a wall. Another thin line of frost ran through Contlay and Emeric, separating them.

"What's this?" Contlay said. "What did you do?"

Jacqueline pounded on the ice barrier, begging to be let in. Contlay slowly walked to the edge of the wall and placed his hand on the ice. He ran his fingers down the side, feeling the smooth, cold texture.

"You killed him," she said, another tear sliding down her cheek. "He had nothing to do with this. He was innocent."

Contlay turned from the wall. "An unexpected casualty. I never meant to hit him. I was aiming for you."

Lana's fingers curled into a fist. She was so angry she couldn't think straight. She clenched her mouth, her teeth grinding into each other. The frost kept building upon itself, until they were standing in an enclosed room. The light permeated the ice, casting sparkles. It was beautiful, but she couldn't let herself get sidetracked.

Jacqueline continued to pound her fist on the wall, trying to break through. Ramos ran his hands along the side, searching for a crack, anything to let him in. Lana could barely make out Grayson, holding off Contlay's army.

"I trusted you. I thought you were one of the good guys."

Contlay's lips curled. "Aren't we all bad guys in somebody's story? The world is full of people trying to survive."

His answer angered her even more. It was an excuse. It may be his narrative, something he told himself to survive the guilt of the horrible things he had done but it wasn't true. It couldn't be true. She was fighting for the good in the world.

Contlay held his hands out, searching for the gun. His hands flew to his pocket. He threw them inside only to remove them a moment later, a frown on his face when he realized he didn't have it.

"Looking for that?" Lana asked, pointing to her right, just beyond the wall of ice.

Contlay's face fell when he saw the gun. Jacqueline followed their gaze and ran to the other side of the wall. She picked it up.

"No matter. I won't need it."

Contlay rushed toward her. He stopped when he was within reach and drew his arm back. He swung, hitting Lana in the chin. She flew backward, nearly tripping over her feet. He advanced on her again but this time she was ready. She ducked, narrowly missing his swing.

"What do you think you'll do if you escape? If you beat me? Now that the Council's after you, it's only a matter of time before you're sent to the Yards."

Lana ignored him, pushing his words out of her mind. He was trying to distract her. He stepped forward before lifting his right leg and swinging it at her. She saw it coming and retreated. When his leg connected with empty air, he stumbled back, the wall of ice preventing him from falling over.

Through the clear barrier, Lana saw Mick behind Jacqueline. Jacqueline was concentrated on their fight, ignoring everything behind her. Lana gestured wildly with her hands, trying to warn her.

Lana's momentary distraction was all Contlay needed. He used it to his advantage and threw her against the wall. She hit it with a loud thud. Jacqueline screamed as dark spots clouded Lana's vision.

"You made this too easy for me," he snarled. "There's no one to help you in here."

He threw himself against her once more. She fell backward and hit her head against the floor. Her breath caught in her throat. She couldn't think clearly. She knew she had to get up. She knew she had to fight but her body didn't want to respond.

His calloused hands wrapped around her neck, his fingers curling around her hair, pressing into her skin. She tried to kick him off. She pressed her leg on his abdomen, but he was too strong. She grunted from the exertion. His fingers pressed deep into her flesh and she struggled to breathe.

Lana heard screaming outside of the ice walls, although she couldn't make out anything that was being said. Her hands flew to her neck. She tried to remove his fingers, to loosen their hold. She struggled for air, her legs kicking wildly. Her eyes began to water. Just when she thought she couldn't take it anymore, Contlay screamed. He loosened his grip just enough for her to roll out from underneath him.

Lana pushed herself up, scrambling to get as far away from him as she could. She struggled for air, the shock overtaking her. Contlay screamed again. A large line of frost had covered his legs and was moving up his body. The ice layered upon itself, covering him completely. He cried out one last time as the frost devoured him. All around her, the ice wall went up in flames.

# 16

# THE ASHES

Lana ran her hand along the dress, searching for something to hold on to. An entire week had passed since they left Ganyon Falls. An entire week without Dominic.

Kiernan took her hand in his, squeezing it softly. She looked up at him. He offered her a weak smile, and she gripped his hand tighter. She wrapped her fingers in his, grateful that he was with her.

"Are we ready?"

Nolan looked at Ramos, waiting to see if he was ready to begin. Ramos nodded. Deliah let out a loud cry before burying her head in his shoulder.

"I suppose we are," Charlotte said. "As ready as we can be."

Nolan nodded. "On behalf of the Morgan family, I would like to thank you all for being here today. King Ramos and Queen Charlotte have received countless support throughout this difficult time and your presence is very much appreciated." Nolan paused, meeting the gaze of each mourner. "I'm sure the King and Queen take comfort in seeing everyone here today, a reminder of the young Prince's impact on so many."

Lana couldn't listen anymore. She didn't think she had

anymore tears left to shed. She hadn't thought her life could get any worse, but somehow it did. The past week felt like a terrible nightmare. Every morning brought new sadness. She would never be the same.

After leaving Ganyon Falls, they made their way back to Bridian. Ramos alerted the Council that Contlay had attacked them. When the ice thawed, they thought he was dead. It had been Emeric that found a low pulse. Contlay, along with his followers, were taken into the Council's custody. Her only regret was that he wasn't dead.

Before reapers were sent to Emeric's, Lana had already left. Ramos informed them that she had vanished. Everyone corroborated his story and she had spent the last week locked in an extra room in the castle. She hadn't even gone to her bedroom for fear someone would see her and alert the Council. She wouldn't be staying long anyway.

Jacqueline and Grayson were going on the run with her. They had wanted to leave immediately but Lana couldn't. Not until Dominic's funeral. She owed him that. She didn't know where they were going and didn't even care. She only hoped she could find the dagger before Alderic.

Kiernan ran his thumb over hers, bringing her back to reality. The past week had been a stark, painful reminder that life was fragile. It was too short to waste. He was one of the few people that knew she was there. They spent the last week together, reminiscing about their time with Dominic and helping Deliah heal.

"As we celebrate the life of Prince Dominic Morgan, we take solace that he's at peace," Nolan finished.

Ramos hugged Charlotte before stepping forward. He carried a large gold urn in his hands. Deliah broke free from Terris and ran to her father. She wrapped her arms around him. Charlotte joined them.

Lana looked away, giving them a small moment of privacy.

She couldn't imagine their grief. Tomorrow they would have a large public funeral, attended by everyone in Bridian. She would be gone by then. She wished she could be there for Deliah.

Her eyes passed over each attendee, wondering if it would be the last time they would be together. Grant stood behind Lana. She wasn't sure what he was going to do if the Council came for her, but it was nice to know he was there, for now. He had asked to come on the run with her, but Jacqueline and Grayson thought it would be too much. The fewer people with her, the better chance they had to stay hidden.

Ramos unscrewed the top of the urn. He passed it to Charlotte, who held it between both her hands. A tear slid down her cheek and she quickly wiped it away. Deliah's eyes were on the grass, as if she couldn't bear to look.

"Until we meet again," Ramos said.

Another soft breeze flew around them, carrying a large orange and black butterfly. When Terris caught her eye, she pointed to it. He followed her gaze and they both watched it flutter toward Ramos and Charlotte, finally settling on Deliah's hand. When she noticed it, the butterfly flew off, following the wind.

"We all return to ash," Nolan said.

Ramos took Charlotte's hand before emptying the urn. The ashes scattered, floating with the wind. Lana couldn't hold back the tears any longer. Nolan's words repeated in her mind, pulling at a memory. *We all return to ash.* The hair on her neck prickled and she gasped.

Kiernan turned to her, narrowing his eyes. "What's wrong?"

Lana shook her head, not wanting to say anything for fear she would lose her train of thought. She closed her eyes, trying to piece it together.

*Protected in ashes.*

Lana concentrated, pushing aside thoughts of everything

else. What was the rest of the Revatto's motto? If they knew how important, how dangerous the dagger could truly be, maybe they hid it somewhere else, other than the caves. Maybe they realized the caves would be the first place someone would think to look? Could their motto be more than just a pledge? Could it be the key to the dagger's hiding place?

*The burden...*

*The darkness...*

As hard as she tried, she couldn't remember the rest of the poem. She opened her eyes, determined to go to her room before they left. The timing would work, she had planned to say goodbye to Trevor and Heidi before she left anyway. They would both be spending some extra time in Bridian, protected at the castle, until they felt safe enough to leave for Mt. Sinclair. Heidi was recovering in a room next to Trevor's.

Lana watched the wildflowers, the sea of oranges, blues, and purples swaying in the breeze. Deep down, she knew she would see Dominic again. She knew there was more than her current life. There had to be. Dominic's last words came back to her. *Don't let the darkness in.* She shivered. It was too late for that. Not only was the darkness in, but it was overpowering her.

Lana wondered if she had even seen Dominic that night or if it was only a response to the trauma. Had she imagined it? She hadn't told anyone else what happened and didn't think anyone would even believe her anyway. The last week she tried to see him again. She had done everything she could think of to make it happen. She meditated, she stopped time, but nothing worked. She hadn't seen the demon either. While she thought her grief would have made her more susceptible to them, they were noticeably quiet. She had almost felt like herself the past week.

"Thank you for being a part of my son's life," Ramos said, looking at everyone. "I know how much you all meant to him.

Physically he may be gone, but we won't let his memory fade. He's in my father's care now."

Lana wiped the last tears from her eyes. She took a deep breath, letting the oxygen clear her head. Deliah walked back to Terris. Lana was glad that they had each other. With Dominic gone, and her leaving, they needed each other.

"Let's make our way to the dining hall," Charlotte said, her voice cracking, the air of confidence absent.

Ramos nodded. "It will just be us, one last meal together before Lana, Jacqueline, and Grayson leave."

Kiernan squeezed her hand again. She didn't look at him. She didn't want to cry again. Besides, she would see him again soon. She was determined to find a way to release the demons, send them home, and convince the Council that she was no longer a threat.

"Are you ready?" she asked.

When he nodded, she took his other hand. She had teleported to the field with Kiernan earlier. She wanted to spend as much time as she could with him before she left. A moment later, they were standing in her bedroom. The room was dark and cold, noticeably devoid of life. When would she see it again?

"Why are we here?" he asked, his head tilted slightly to the right.

Lana's eyes darted across the room. "I just have to find something."

When she saw the book on the floor, she ran to it. She flipped through the pages, trying to remember where the poem was. Her hands shook when she found the page. She brought it close, reading the words in the dark.

*The burden is heavy,*
*The darkness within,*
*From this day forward,*

*Protected in ashes.*

Lana reread the poem three times, memorizing each word. When she felt that she had successfully memorized it, she placed the book on the floor. She pointed out the poem for Kiernan.

"I think this is about the dagger."

Kiernan leaned closer, reading the words. When he finished, he looked back at her. "The Revatto's motto. It's about their duty to protect the Medoran Royal Family."

"It's about the dagger," Lana said. "I think they passed it off as their duty, but it was their way of making sure the knowledge was preserved, that future generations of Revatto knew where to find it, to keep it hidden."

"So, protected in ashes," Kiernan said. "Where do you think it is?"

Lana shook her head. "I don't know, but I'll figure it out."

She closed the book. She thought about taking it with her, but knew she needed to pack light. They would be on the run, most likely moving from place to place. It would be one more thing she would have to carry with her.

She stood up quickly, turning to face him. "Ready to go?"

"Not yet," he said.

Kiernan looked into her eyes. Her heart skipped a beat, and her stomach flipped. She could look into his eyes forever. He took her hands again, pulling her to him. They were so close she felt his breath on her cheek, and she shivered.

"I'll be waiting for you," he said.

Lana nodded. She couldn't talk even if she wanted to. Her heart was beating so fast she was worried she would faint. He leaned down, his lips brushing against hers softly. She closed her eyes, losing herself in his kiss. She wrapped her arms around his neck, pulling him closer.

A moment later, he pulled away. He placed his forehead on hers and they stood in silence, trying to catch their breath. Lana wished the moment would never end. She didn't want to leave him.

The sound of the clock chiming the hour broke the moment. He pulled away but still held her hands.

"I wish I could go with you," he said.

"Me too."

"As much as I hate to say this," he said. "We should go. Everyone's probably back by now."

Lana looked around her room one last time, making sure there wasn't anything else she needed to take, when she remembered Trevor.

"There's someone else I have to say goodbye to."

He nodded, looking at the necklace at her throat. "I'll go first. I'll let you know when it's safe."

She wrapped her arms around herself. Kiernan made his way toward the door. He slowly opened it and slipped into the hall. A moment later, he waved that it was clear.

Lana closed the door behind her. A small part of her thought it would be the last time she would ever see her room. As much as she tried to push the voice away, to silence it, it persisted.

Trevor was sitting on his bed. Heidi was sitting in a chair next to him. His face was red, his eyes puffy. Even though Heidi looked exhausted, she radiated happiness. She stood when Lana entered.

"How are you?" she asked.

Lana looked at the ground. How was she supposed to answer? Did Heidi want the real answer? She was terrible. Heidi saw her consternation and wrapped her in a tight hug. She ran her hand down her back, comforting her.

"Thank you," Heidi said. "For always being there for Trevor. You're a good friend. I know things are hard right now, I know it seems like there isn't an end in sight, but everything will be okay."

Lana nodded, fresh tears pooling at her eyes. "I'm just glad you're all right. Trevor was so worried. We all were."

Heidi sniffled. "We're going to stay here for a bit. I don't feel safe at home. He broke in. I had just gotten home from work. I thought it was Trevor at first. You hear stories, you don't actually think it'll happen to you."

Lana nodded. "Will you send a message to Ava? Let her know what happened?" she asked Trevor.

"I already did," he answered. "Your parents helped me."

Lana should have known they would have taken care of it. She shifted on her feet. She hated goodbyes.

Trevor stood. He slowly made his way to her. Heidi took his arm, helping him. When he reached Lana, he hugged her.

"I'll see you soon."

"Maybe I'll figure this out quickly," she said. "Maybe I'll be back before you leave?"

Trevor stepped back, leaning against his mom again. "I hope so."

They stood in silence for a moment. The unspoken words hanging in the air, on the tip of their tongues. Lana bit her bottom lip, using it as a distraction. She didn't want to think that this may be the last time she may see him. The fact that she may never see Ava again.

"We should go," Lana said. "Everyone's probably wondering where I am."

"Stay safe," Heidi said.

Kiernan stepped closer to Lana, taking her hands. She smiled at Trevor one last time before closing her eyes, envisioning the dining hall. When she opened her eyes, she saw they were exactly where she had pictured, behind a large curtain that blocked the staff door. She wanted to be sure that it was safe before making her presence known.

"Where is she?" Grayson asked. "Should we check her room? You don't think she left without us?"

"She wouldn't do that," Jacqueline said, her voice steady. "She's probably saying goodbye to Kiernan in private."

Lana looked up at Kiernan. She never wanted to forget their kiss. He smiled. She stepped around the curtain before she lost her nerve.

"See, I told you," Jacqueline said, noticing Lana. "We're going to leave shortly. They're packing our food to go."

"Is everything okay? I thought we would get to eat together. One last time."

"This has been a gamble to begin with," Grayson said. "It's better if we leave as soon as we can."

Lana looked around the room, her eyes darting to her friends and family. How was she supposed to leave them? How was she supposed to leave Deliah? Her cousin was hurting, and she was leaving. It wasn't right. It didn't feel right.

When she saw Ramos, she remembered Dominic's request. He wanted her to tell his parents that he loved them. He had asked her to take care of Deliah. Even if it hadn't been real, even if it had only been her imagination, she was going to tell them.

"I need a minute," she said. "I want to say goodbye."

"Of course," Jacqueline said.

Deliah was sitting at her usual seat. Terris was next to her, in Dominic's chair. She quickly walked to them. Deliah didn't even look up. She was hunched over the table, looking at her hands.

"Deliah," Lana began. "Nothing I say will make this better. I'm so sorry."

Deliah didn't move. "I know."

Lana placed her hand on her cousin's. She wished she could take her pain away. She wished she could make her feel better.

"I'm leaving," Lana said. "I'll be back as soon as I can."

Deliah eyes were red and puffy. Even though she was looking at Lana, it didn't seem as if she was actually seeing anything. Her expression was vacant. She looked lost.

"How am I supposed to do this? Dom's always been here. I don't know how I'm supposed to do this without him."

Deliah's words struck Lana numb. She didn't know how she was supposed to answer. She didn't know how to process her own grief, and it was nothing compared to Deliah's.

"You're not alone," Terris said. "We're here for you. We'll help."

Deliah turned away. Lana reached out to hug her cousin. "I'll be back soon."

When Deliah didn't answer, Lana made her way to Terris. He stood and she hugged him. Her stomach lurched at the thought of leaving him.

"Take care of her," she whispered.

"Of course," he said, squeezing her tighter. "I'll see you soon."

Lana wiped her face, trying to hold back the tears. She made her way to Ramos at the head of the table. He sat with his head in his hands. Before she could reach him, Grant walked into the room. He closed the door behind him and looked up, meeting her eyes and approached her.

"I'll miss you," he said.

Lana smiled. "What are you going to do with all your free time?"

He chuckled. "Stay safe. You know where to find me."

Lana proceeded to Ramos. Charlotte wasn't in the room. Her uncle would be her last goodbye. She swallowed the lump in her throat and sat next to him. The movement made him look up. His eyes were heavy and the skin underneath his lower lashes was thin, lined with deep bags.

"I'm so sorry," she said.

"My worst nightmare was that Alderic would escape the

Yards, that he would come back into my life," Ramos began. "I didn't realize the real nightmare of losing a child. And I lost two."

Lana choked back tears. She didn't want to cry again. She didn't want to set him off. It wasn't fair. She didn't understand the evil in the world. She didn't understand how bad things happened to good people. Ramos didn't deserve this. Deliah didn't deserve this. Dominic didn't deserve to die. He had his whole life ahead of him.

"I saw him," she said, wiping a tear from under her eye. "I don't know how. I don't even know if I imagined it. He said it was always meant to be this way. He wanted me to tell you that he loves you. He wanted me to tell Charlotte that he loves her. He wanted me to look after Deliah."

His eyes met hers. "When?"

"Right after he was shot. Time had stopped. He was there. The brightest light was around him. He said I could see him because the magic makes me vibrate higher...whatever that means. I should have told you sooner, but I don't know if it even happened. I may have imagined it."

He smiled. "Always thinking about his family. My boy—"

The tears poured out of him. He reached for a napkin and held it to his mouth. Before Lana could do anything, the doors slammed open, and something pierced her back. She cried out in pain before falling to the floor.

"What is this?" Ramos stood, the anger radiating out of him.

Lana's eyes were heavy. She tried to move. She tried to stand but couldn't. She heard Jacqueline next to her.

"Take her," a familiar voice said.

Waves of nausea rolled through her. The lights mutated, melting together. The colors were blinding. The floor vibrated, and a pair of hands wrapped around her.

"You can't do this," Ramos said. "You're in my kingdom."

A figure came closer to Lana. She squinted, the face coming

into view. Gideon. He smiled at her before turning back to Ramos.

"You forget your place," he said. "The Council supersedes all."

"This isn't right," Jacqueline said, scrambling to reach Lana. "We'll take responsibility for her."

"That won't be necessary," Gideon said, turning back to Ramos. "I am sorry about your son."

The reaper holding Lana began walking. She tried to teleport, she tried to stop time, but nothing worked. Whatever they injected her with was inhibiting the magic. She lifted her arm, trying to hit the man, hoping he would release her.

"Don't waste your energy," Gideon said, his face coming into focus before her. "You'll need it in the Yards."

Lana's eyes grew heavy. She tried to keep them open, she tried to fight. As the poison spread, her vision blurred and her muscles contracted, involuntarily spasming before falling limp. She succumbed to the darkness, violet flames filling her vision, turning everything to ash.

# ALSO BY JESSICA LEMORE

The Mirrored Crown Series (Young Adult Fantasy)

The Princess of the Rebellion

The Crystal of Medora

The Darkness Within

The Shadow Marked Series (New Adult Fantasy Romance)

Curse of Lies and Shadow

Curse of Darkness and Desire: Coming Soon

If you've enjoyed this book, please leave a review!

# ABOUT THE AUTHOR

Jessica R. LeMore is the author of *The Mirrored Crown* series. She lives in Upstate New York with her husband and son. You can visit her online at www.jessicarlemore.com.